PENGUIN CLASSICS

Maigret, Lognon and the

'Extraordinary masterpieces of the twentieth century'
– John Banville

'A brilliant writer'   – India Knight

'Intense atmosphere and resonant detail . . . make Simenon's
fiction remarkably like life'   – Julian Barnes

'A truly wonderful writer . . . marvellously readable – lucid,
simple, absolutely in tune with the world he creates'
– Muriel Spark

'Few writers have ever conveyed with such a sure touch, the
bleakness of human life'   – A. N. Wilson

'Compelling, remorseless, brilliant'   – John Gray

'A writer of genius, one whose simplicity of language creates
indelible images that the florid stylists of our own day can
only dream of'   – *Daily Mail*

'The mysteries of the human personality are revealed in all
their disconcerting complexity'   – Anita Brookner

'One of the greatest writers of our time'
– *The Sunday Times*

'I love reading Simenon. He makes me think of Chekhov'
– William Faulkner

'One of the great psychological novelists of this century'
– *Independent*

'The greatest of all, the most genuine novelist we have had
in literature'   – André Gide

'Simenon ought to be spoken of in the same breath as
Camus, Beckett and Kafka'   – *Independent on Sunday*

GEORGES SIMENON

Maigret, Lognon and the Gangsters

Translated by WILLIAM HOBSON

PENGUIN BOOKS

PENGUIN CLASSICS

UK | USA | Canada | Ireland | Australia
India | New Zealand | South Africa

Penguin Books is part of the Penguin Random House group of companies
whose addresses can be found at global.penguinrandomhouse.com

Penguin
Random House
UK

First published in French as *Maigret, Lognon et les gangsters* by Presses de la Cité 1952
This translation first published 2017
006

Copyright © Georges Simenon Limited, 1952
Translation copyright © William Hobson, 2017
GEORGES SIMENON ® Simenon.tm
MAIGRET ® Georges Simenon Limited
All rights reserved

Set in Dante MT Std 12.5/15pt
Typeset in India by Thomson Digital Pvt Ltd, Noida, Delhi
Printed and bound in Great Britain by Clays Ltd, Elcograf S.p.A.

ISBN: 978-0-241-25066-2

www.greenpenguin.co.uk

MIX
Paper from
responsible sources
FSC® C018179

Penguin Random House is committed to a
sustainable future for our business, our readers
and our planet. This book is made from Forest
Stewardship Council® certified paper.

Maigret, Lognon and the Gangsters

1.

In which Maigret has to deal with Madame Lognon with her infirmities and her gangsters

'All right ... All right ... Yes ... Of course ... Of course ... I promise I'll do everything I can. That's right ... Goodbye ... What? ... I said goodbye ... No offence taken ... Good day, monsieur ...'

For what was probably the tenth time, although he had given up counting, Maigret hung up the telephone, relit his pipe with a reproachful look at the long, cold rain falling outside his window and, grabbing his pen, bent over the report he had begun an hour earlier, which was still less than half a page long.

As he began writing again, he was actually thinking about something else. He was thinking about the rain, that particular rain before winter really sets in which has a way of getting down your neck and into your shoes, of sluicing off your hat in big drops, a rain for head colds, grimy and dreary, that makes people want to stay at home, where they linger at their windows like ghosts.

Is it boredom then that makes them ring up? Of the eight or ten telephone calls, more or less in succession, not even three were of any use. And now it was ringing again.

Maigret looked at the telephone as if he wanted to smash it to pieces with his fist, then finally barked:

'Hello?'

'Madame Lognon insists on talking to you personally.'

'Madame who?'

'Lognon.'

In this weather, when he was already feeling exasperated, Maigret thought it must be a practical joke, suddenly hearing the name of the police officer nicknamed Inspector Hard-Done-By on the other end of the line: Lognon, the most lugubrious individual in the entire Parisian police force, a man whose bad luck was so proverbial some people claimed he was cursed.

It wasn't even Lognon on the telephone but Madame Lognon. Maigret had only met her once, at their apartment on Place Constantin-Pecqueur in Montmartre, but since then he no longer bore the inspector any hard feelings. He still gave him a wide berth but now pitied him with all his heart.

'Put her on . . . Hello, Madame Lognon?'

'I apologize for disturbing you, detective chief inspector . . .'

She articulated every syllable in that affected way people do when they want to impress on you that they have received a good education. Maigret noted that it was Thursday, 19 November. The black marble clock on the mantelpiece showed eleven in the morning.

'I wouldn't have taken the liberty of insisting on speaking to you personally if I didn't have a most urgent reason . . .'

'Yes, madame.'

'You know us, my husband and I. You know that . . .'

'Yes, madame.'

'I absolutely must see you, inspector. Horrible things are happening, and I'm frightened. If my health didn't prevent me, I would rush straight to Quai des Orfèvres. But, as you know, I have been confined to this fifth floor of mine for years now.'

'If I understand you correctly, you would like me to come there?'

'Please will you, Monsieur Maigret?'

This was quite something. Her request was polite but firm.

'Isn't your husband at home?'

'He has disappeared.'

'What? Lognon's disappeared? Since when?'

'I don't know. He's not in his office, and no one knows where he is. The gangsters came back this morning.'

'The what?'

'The gangsters. I'll tell you everything. If Lognon is furious, then so be it. I am too frightened.'

'Do you mean that people have been in your apartment?'

'Yes.'

'Did they force their way in?'

'Yes.'

'While you were there?'

'Yes.'

'Did they take anything?'

'Possibly some papers. I haven't been able to check.'

'Did this happen this morning?'

'Half an hour ago. But the other two had already come the day before yesterday.'

'How did your husband react?'

'I haven't set eyes on him since.'

'I'm on my way.'

Maigret wasn't convinced. Not entirely. He scratched his head, chose a couple of pipes, which he slipped into his pocket, then half-opened the door to the inspectors' office.

'Anyone heard any news of Lognon lately?'

That name always brought a smile to everyone's lips, but no, no one had heard anything about him. Despite his burning ambition to be part of Quai des Orfèvres, Inspector Lognon in fact belonged to the second district of the ninth arrondissement, and his office was in Rue de la Rochefoucauld station.

'If anyone asks for me, I'll be back in an hour. Is there a car downstairs?'

He put on his bulky overcoat, found a small police car in the courtyard and gave the address on Place Constantin-Pecqueur. It was as cheery out in the streets as under Gare du Nord's glass dome, and pedestrians soldiered on, their legs drenched by the jets of dirty water the cars were spraying over the pavements.

The Lognons' building was a nondescript, century-old apartment block without a lift. Maigret climbed the five storeys, sighing. Finally a door opened without his needing to knock, and Madame Lognon, her eyes and nose red, let him in, murmuring:

'I am so grateful to you for coming! If you only knew how much my poor husband admires you.'

This wasn't true. Lognon loathed him. Lognon loathed everyone who was lucky enough to work at Quai des Orfèvres, every detective chief inspector, every officer of a higher rank than him . . . He loathed the older officers for being older than him and the younger officers for their youth. He . . .

'Sit down, inspector . . .'

She was short and thin, with messy hair, and she was wearing a flannel dressing gown in a hideous shade of mauve. There were dark rings under her eyes, her nostrils were pinched, and she constantly brought her hand to the left side of her chest like someone with a bad heart.

'I thought it best not to touch anything, so you could see for yourself . . .'

The apartment was cramped: dining room, living room, bedroom, kitchen and bathroom, all so small the furniture prevented you from opening the doors completely. On the bed a black cat was curled into a ball.

Madame Lognon had shown Maigret into the dining room, and it was obvious the living room was never used. Rather than silver, the sideboard was full of papers, books and photographs, and its drawers had been ransacked. Letters were strewn across the floor.

'I think,' he said, unsure whether to light his pipe, 'that you'd better begin at the beginning. You mentioned gangsters just now on the telephone.'

By way of introduction, she said in the resigned tones of the long-suffering:

'You may smoke your pipe.'

'Thank you.'

'You see, since Tuesday morning . . .'

'That's to say, the day before yesterday?'

'Yes. This week Lognon is on night shift. On Tuesday morning he came home just after six o'clock, as usual. But instead of going to bed straight after a bite to eat, he paced around the apartment for over an hour until I felt dizzy.'

'Did he seem worried?'

'You know how conscientious he is, inspector. I am always telling him he is too conscientious: he is ruining his health, and no one ever shows him a blind bit of gratitude for it. Forgive me for speaking so frankly, but you must admit that he has never been treated as he deserves. All he thinks about is his work, he worries himself sick . . .'

'So, on Tuesday morning . . .'

'At eight, he went to the market to do the shopping. I am ashamed to be no better than a helpless woman, practically good for nothing, but it isn't my fault. The doctor has forbidden me to use the stairs, and so of course Lognon has to buy what we need. It's no job for a man like him, I know. Every time, I . . .'

'On Tuesday morning . . . ?'

'He did the shopping. Then he told me that he had to go to the office, that he probably wouldn't be long and that he would have a sleep in the afternoon.'

'Did he talk about the case he was working on?'

'He never does that. If I ever make the mistake of asking him about it, he'll say he is bound by professional confidentiality.'

'Did he come back afterwards?'

'Yes, around eleven.'

'The same day?'

'Yes. Tuesday, around eleven in the morning.'

'Was he still on edge?'

'I don't know if he was on edge or if it was his cold, because he had caught a head cold. I insisted he took something. He told me he would take something later, when he had time, that now he had to go out again, but that he would be back before dinner.'

'Did he come home?'

'Wait. My God, I've suddenly thought of something! What if I never see him again? And to think of how I reproached him, telling him that he didn't care about his wife, only his work . . .'

Maigret waited with a resigned air, perched awkwardly on a chair with an uncomfortably straight back, which was too flimsy for him to dare tip back.

'Maybe a quarter of an hour after he left, or perhaps not even that, around one o'clock, I heard footsteps on the stairs. I assumed they were going up to her on the sixth floor, a woman who, between ourselves . . .'

'Yes. Footsteps on the stairs . . .'

'They stopped on my landing. I had just gone back to bed, as the doctor ordered me to do after meals. There was a knock on the door, which I didn't answer. Lognon has advised me never to answer when people don't say who they are. You can't do the sort of work he does without having enemies, can you? I was amazed when I heard the door opening, then footsteps in the hall, then in the dining room. There were two of them, two men who looked into the bedroom and saw me, still in bed.'

'Could you get a good look at them?'

'I told them to go away, threatened to call the police. I even reached out a hand to the telephone, which is on the bedside table.'

'And then?'

'One of the two, the shorter one, showed me his gun, saying something in a language I didn't understand, probably English.'

'What did they look like?'

'I don't know how to put it. They were very well dressed. Both of them were smoking cigarettes. They had kept their hats on. They seemed surprised not to find something or someone.

'"If it is my husband you want to see . . ." I started.

'But they weren't listening. The taller one went round the apartment, while the other watched me. I remember that they looked under the bed, in the wardrobes.'

'They didn't search the chest of drawers?'

'Those two didn't, no. They barely stayed five minutes, didn't ask me anything, then quietly left as if their visit was perfectly normal. Of course, I rushed to the window and I saw them talking on the pavement next to a big black car. The taller one got in, and the other walked to the corner of Rue Caulaincourt, where I think he went into the bar. I immediately rang my husband's office.'

'Was he there?'

'Yes. He had just arrived. I told him what had happened.'

'Did he seem surprised?'

'It is hard to say. He always sounds strange on the telephone.'

'Did he ask you to describe the two men?'

'Yes. I did.'

'Do so again.'

'They were both very dark, like Italians, but I'm sure what they were speaking wasn't Italian. I think the one in charge was the tall one – a handsome man, I must say, just a shade overweight, in his forties. He looked as if he had come straight from the barber's.'

'And the short one?'

'Coarser, with a broken nose and boxer's ears and a gold front tooth. He was wearing a pearl-grey hat and a grey coat, the other one a brand new camel hair coat.'

'Did your husband come straight home?'

'No.'

'Didn't he send anyone from the local station?'

'He didn't do that either. He told me I wasn't to worry, even if he didn't come home for a few days. I asked him what I would do for food, and he said that he would take care of it.'

'Did he?'

'Yes. The following morning, the local shops delivered what I needed. They came by again this morning.'

'Did you hear from Lognon yesterday, during the day?'

'He telephoned me twice.'

'And today?'

'Once, around nine o'clock.'

'Do you know where he called you from?'

'No. He never tells me where he is. I don't know how the other inspectors are with their wives, but he . . .'

'Let's move on to this morning's visit.'

'I heard footsteps on the stairs again.'

'What time?'

'Just after ten. I didn't look at the alarm clock. Perhaps ten thirty.'

'Was it the same men?'

'There was only one, and I had never seen him before. He did not knock, just marched straight in as if he had a key. Perhaps he used a master key? I was in the kitchen, peeling my vegetables. I got up from my chair and saw him in the doorway.

'"Don't move," he said to me. "Whatever you do, don't scream. I'm not going to hurt you."'

'Did he have an accent?'

'Yes. He made some mistakes in his French. This one looked like a typical American, I'm sure: tall, with blond, almost red, hair and broad shoulders, and he was chewing gum. He looked around curiously, as if it was the first time he had seen a Parisian apartment. The moment he glanced in the sitting room, he spotted the certificate Lognon was awarded for twenty-five years' service.'

The certificate, enclosed in a black wooden frame with gold inlay, had Lognon's name and rank written in round hand.

'"A cop, eh," the man said to me. "Where is he?"'

'I said that I didn't know, which did not seem to bother him in the slightest. Then he started opening drawers, going through the papers and throwing them back any old how, so that they sometimes fell on the floor. He found a photograph of the two of us taken fifteen years ago. He looked up at me, nodding his head, then put the photo in his pocket.'

'Basically, he didn't seem to be expecting that your husband would be in the police?'

'He wasn't particularly surprised, but I'm convinced that he didn't know when he got here.'

'Did he ask you what unit he was in?'

'He asked me where he could find him. I said I had no idea, my husband never talked to me about his work.'

'He didn't push it?'

'He kept on reading whatever he could get his hands on.'

'Was your husband's police accreditation in the drawer?'

'Yes. The man put some of the documents in his pocket with the photo. Then he found a bottle of calvados on the top shelf of the sideboard and poured himself a large glass.'

'That's all?'

'He looked under the bed, like the others, and in the two cupboards. He went back to have another drink in the dining room and then he left with a mocking little wave.'

'Did you notice if he was wearing gloves?'

'Pigskin gloves, yes.'

'And the other two?'

'I think they had gloves on as well. At any rate, the one who threatened me with his gun did.'

'Did you go to the window again?'

'Yes. I saw him leave the building and join one of the two others, the short one, who was waiting for him on the corner of Rue Caulaincourt. I immediately called Rue de La Rochefoucauld station and asked to speak to Lognon. They told me that he hadn't been seen that morning and that they weren't expecting him. When I insisted, they told me that he hadn't been into the office the night before, even though he was on duty.'

'Did you tell them what had happened?'

'No. I immediately thought of you, inspector. You see, I know Lognon better than anyone. He is the sort of person who's obsessed with doing the right thing. So far he has never had the recognition he deserves, but he has often talked about you. I know you're not like the others, you don't envy him, you . . . I'm frightened, Monsieur Maigret. He must have gone after people stronger than him and by now, God knows where . . .'

The telephone rang in the bedroom.

Madame Lognon started.

'May I?'

Maigret heard her, suddenly tight-lipped, saying, 'What? Is that you? Where were you? I rang your office, and they told me that you hadn't set foot in there since yesterday. Detective Chief Inspector Maigret is here . . .'

Maigret, who had followed her, stretched out a hand for the receiver.

'Do you mind? . . . Hello, Lognon?'

Lognon remained silent on the other end of the line, with a fixed stare, no doubt, his teeth clenched.

'Tell me, Lognon, where are you at the moment?'

'At the office.'

'I'm in your apartment with your wife. I need to speak to you. I'll drop by Rue de La Rochefoucauld, it's on my way. Wait for me . . . What?'

'I'd rather we didn't meet here. I'll explain . . .' he heard Lognon stammer.

'Be at Quai des Orfèvres in half an hour then.'

He hung up the telephone and went and fetched his pipe and hat.

'Do you think everything is all right?'

He looked at her uncomprehendingly, so she went on:

'He's so reckless, so single-minded, that sometimes . . .'

'Send him in.'

Lognon was soaked and muddy, as if he had been roaming the streets all night, and he had such a bad cold that he had to have his handkerchief constantly in his hand. He tilted his head to one side, like someone expecting to be taken to task, and stayed standing in the middle of the room.

'Sit down, Lognon. I've just come from your apartment.'

'What did my wife tell you?'

'Everything she knows, I suppose.'

There followed a fairly long silence, which Lognon took advantage of to blow his nose, without daring to look Maigret in the face. Knowing how touchy he was, Maigret wasn't sure exactly what approach to take.

What Madame Lognon had said about her husband wasn't so far off the mark. In his desire to do the right thing, that halfwit was always getting into scrapes, convinced that the whole world was against him, that he was the victim of a conspiracy to prevent him being promoted and finally assuming his rightful place in the Crime Squad at Quai des Orfèvres.

What was most distressing was that he wasn't stupid, he was genuinely conscientious and he was the most honest man on earth.

'Is she in bed?' he asked finally.

'She was up when I got there.'

'Is she angry with me?'

'Look at me, Lognon. Relax. All I know is what your wife has told me, but I only have to take one look at you to know something's wrong. I'm not your immediate superior, so whatever you've done is none of my concern. But perhaps, now your wife has spoken to me, you'd better fill me in. What do you think?'

'I think I should, yes.'

'In that case, please tell me everything. Do you understand? Not just a part, not *almost* everything.'

'I understand.'

'Good. You can smoke.'

'I don't smoke.'

It was true. Maigret had forgotten. He didn't smoke because of Madame Lognon, whom the smell of tobacco made nauseous.

'What do you know about these gangsters?'

'I think they really are gangsters,' Lognon said emphatically.

'American?'

'Yes.'

'How did you come into contact with them?'

'I don't really know myself. After what I've been through, I might as well tell you everything, even if it means losing my job.'

He stared fixedly at the desk, his lower lip quivering.

'It would have happened sooner or later anyway.'

'What would have?'

'You know very well. They keep me on because they've got no choice, they haven't caught me out yet, but they've been watching me for years . . .'

'Who?'

'Everyone.'

'For goodness sake, Lognon!'

'Yes, inspector.'

'Will you stop playing the victim?'

'I'm sorry.'

'Stop hunching your shoulders and looking off in the other direction. Good! Now, talk to me like a man.'

Lognon wasn't crying, but his cold was making his eyes water, and it was irritating seeing him constantly bringing his handkerchief to his face.

'I'm listening.'

'It was on Monday night.'

'Were you on duty?'

'Yes. It was about one in the morning. I was on a stakeout.'

'Where?'

'Near the church of Notre-Dame-de-Lorette, right by the railings, on the corner of Rue Fléchier.'

'So you weren't in your sector?'

'Just on the edge. Rue Fléchier is in the third district, but I was watching the little bar at the corner of Rue des Martyrs, which is in my patch. I'd had a tip-off that a guy sometimes went there at night to sell cocaine. Rue Fléchier is dark, almost always empty at that time. I was standing right by the railings round the church. Suddenly a car turned the corner of Rue de Châteaudun, slowed down and pulled up for a moment less than ten metres away from me. The people inside didn't suspect I was there. The door opened, and a body was thrown on the pavement; then the car set off again towards Rue Saint-Lazare.'

'Did you get its number?'

'Yes. I rushed over to the body first. I'd almost swear the man was dead, but I am not completely sure. I felt his chest in the dark, and my hand came away sticky with warm blood.'

Frowning, Maigret muttered:

'I didn't see anything about this in the report.'

'I know.'

'This happened on Rue Fléchier, so on the pavement in the third district.'

'Yes.'

'How is it that . . .'

'I am going to tell you. I know I was wrong. Maybe you won't believe me.'

'What happened to the body?'

'Exactly. I'm getting to that. There wasn't a policeman anywhere. The little bar was open, less than a hundred metres away. I went there to telephone.'

'Who?'

'The station in the third district.'

'Did you?'

'I stopped at the bar to ask for a token. I automatically glanced at the street and saw a second car leaving Rue Fléchier, speeding off down Rue Notre-Dame-de-Lorette. It had stopped near where I'd left the body. I ran out of the bar to try to see the number, but the car was already too far away.'

'A taxi?'

'I don't think so. It all happened so fast. I had a hunch and ran towards the church. The body wasn't there, by the railings.'

'Didn't you raise the alarm?'

'No.'

'Didn't it occur to you that by putting out the number of the first car the police would have a chance of catching it?'

'I thought that. But it seemed to me that the men involved weren't stupid enough to drive around in the same car for very long.'

'You didn't file a report?'

Maigret had, of course, understood. Poor Lognon had been waiting for the big case that would put him in the limelight for years. Bad luck really did seem to follow him around. His sector had one of the heaviest crime rates, but every time a crime was committed either he wasn't on duty or the Crime Squad would take over the investigation.

'I know it was wrong of me. I realized almost immediately but, because I hadn't given the alarm, it was already too late.'

'Did you find the car?'

'I went to the Préfecture in the morning, checked the lists and found out the car was from a garage in Porte Maillot. It's a place that hires out cars without a driver by the day or the month.'

'Had the car been returned?'

'No. It had been rented two days earlier for an unspecified amount of time. I saw the customer card: someone called Bill Larner, an American citizen, resident at the Hôtel Wagram, Avenue Wagram.'

'Did you find Larner there?'

'He had left the hotel around four in the morning.'

'You mean he was in his room until then?'

'Yes.'

'So he wasn't in the car?'

'Definitely not. The night porter saw him come in around midnight. Larner got a telephone call at three thirty and left almost immediately.'

'With his luggage?'

'No. On his way out he said he was going to pick up a friend at the train station and that he would be back for breakfast.'

'Of course he hasn't come back.'

'No.'

'What about the car?'

'It was found the next morning near Gare du Nord.'

Lognon blew his nose again, then looked at Maigret contritely.

'It was wrong of me, I'll say it again. Today's Thursday, and I have been trying since Tuesday morning to put it right. I haven't gone home.'

'Why?'

'My wife must have told you that they came on Tuesday not long after I left. It's a clue, isn't it?'

Maigret listened.

'In my opinion, it means that, after throwing the body on the pavement, they saw me in the shadows. They thought that I must have taken down the number – I mean the number of the first car, of course, because there were two. They dumped it as soon as they could. Then they telephoned Bill Larner, knowing we would probably pick up his trail from the customer card at the garage.'

Maigret was doodling on his blotter as he listened.

'And then?'

'I don't know. I'm just speculating. They must have combed through the newspapers and not found any mention of the business.'

'Do you have an idea how they found you?'

'I can only think of one explanation, which would prove they're very good, these people, professionals. That is that they were waiting near the garage, saw me arrive to make inquiries, then followed me. I went home for lunch and when I left they broke into the apartment.'

'Where they hoped to find the body?'

'Do you think so too?'

'I don't know . . . Why haven't you been back home since?'

'Because I assume they're watching the house.'

'Afraid, Lognon?'

Lognon's cheeks turned as red as his bulbous nose.

'I thought people would think that. But it's not true. I just wanted to be free to move around. I took a room in a little hotel on Place Clichy and kept in touch with my wife by telephone. Since then I've been working day and night. I've visited over a hundred hotels, in the Quartier des Ternes first, then around Avenue de Wagram, then over by Opéra. My wife described the two men who came to the apartment. I went to the immigration bureau at the Préfecture. At the same time, I have been doing all my usual work.'

'So, in a nutshell, you hoped to conduct this investigation by yourself?'

'At first, yes. I thought I was up to it. Now they'll do whatever they want with me.'

Poor Lognon! There were moments when, for all his forty-seven years and unprepossessing appearance, he seemed like a sulky kid, a kid at an awkward age giving the grown-ups aggressive, shifty looks.

'Your wife received a second visit this morning and, as she couldn't reach you, she called me.'

Lognon gave Maigret a despondent look, as if to say that he had reached a point where nothing mattered to him any more.

'It wasn't one of the two men from Tuesday, but a tall man with blond, almost red hair . . .'

'Bill Larner,' muttered Lognon. 'That's how he was described to me.'

'He met up with one of the other two downstairs. He pocketed a photo of you, and probably some papers too.'

'I suppose I'm going to be up before the disciplinary board?'

'There'll be time to discuss that afterwards.'

'After what?'

'After the investigation.'

Lognon frowned, grim-faced, his eyes disbelieving.

'The first thing to do now is to find these characters, don't you think?'

'You mean me too?'

Maigret didn't reply, and Lognon blew his nose for at least three minutes.

When he left the office, anyone would have sworn he had been crying.

2.

In which, although disreputable characters are involved, Inspector Lognon is intent on showing he has good manners

It was almost five o'clock when Maigret's call went through. The lights had been switched on long before, and the floors were wet and muddy from the day's visitors. Did tobacco really taste different in weather like that or was it Maigret's turn to come down with a cold?

He heard the operator say in English, pronouncing his name as if it ended in at least three *t*s:

'Police Judiciaire, Paris. Detective Chief Inspector Maigret calling.'

Then straight afterwards he heard the boyish, ebullient, warm-hearted tones of J. J. MacDonald:

'Hello, Jules!'

Maigret had more or less got used to the American way of doing things by the end of his tour of the United States, but it still went against the grain, and he had to take a deep breath before replying:

'Hello, Jimmy!'

MacDonald was one of the chief right-hand men of J. Edgar Hoover, the head of the FBI in Washington. He had shown Maigret around most of the American cities. He was a tall fellow with light eyes, who generally had his tie in his pocket and his jacket on his arm.

Over there everyone was on first-name terms after ten minutes.

'How's Paris?'

'It's raining.'

'We've got glorious sunshine here.'

'Listen, Jimmy, I need some information and I wouldn't want to waste any taxpayers' money. First, have you heard of someone called Bill Larner?'

'*Sweet* Bill?'

'I don't know. All I've got is the name Bill Larner. Judging by his appearance, he'd be in his forties.'

'It's probably him. He left the country about two years ago and he spent a few months in Havana before sailing for Europe.'

'Dangerous?'

'Not a killer, if that's what you mean, but one of the best conmen going. There's no one like him at swindling an innocent out of fifty dollars by promising him a million. So, he's in your part of the world, is he?'

'He's in Paris.'

'Maybe French law will allow you to nab him. We've never been able to pin enough on him and we've always had to let him go. Do you want me to get a copy of his file sent over?'

'If you can. That's not all though. I'm going to read you a list of names. Stop me if you know any.'

Maigret had set Janvier to work. The Police Judiciaire had compiled a list of all the passengers who had landed at Le Havre and Cherbourg in the last few weeks, then the passport inspectors had given them enough information to eliminate a certain number of names.

'Can you hear me all right?'

'As if you were in the next office.'

MacDonald stopped his French colleague when he was only on the tenth name.

'Did you say Cinaglia?'

'Charles Cinaglia.'

'He's over there too?'

'He turned up two weeks ago.'

'You'd be well advised to keep an eye on him. He's been in prison five or six times. If he'd got what he deserved, he'd have been sent to the electric chair a long time ago. He's a killer. Unfortunately we've only ever been able to get him on illegal possession of firearms, assault and battery, vagrancy, that sort of thing.'

'What does he look like?'

'Short, stocky, always immaculately dressed, diamond ring on his finger, stacked heels. Broken nose and cauliflower ears.'

'He seems to have arrived at the same time as someone called Cicero, who had the cabin next to his.'

'Lord! Tony Cicero worked with Charlie in St Louis. But he doesn't get his hands dirty, as you'd say. He's the brains.'

'Have you got any information on them?'

'Enough to start a library. I'll send you the highlights. And some photos. They'll go out on the evening plane.'

The other names didn't mean anything to MacDonald, and, after another exchange of 'Jules' and 'Jimmy',

Maigret's voice ceased reverberating around a sunlit office in Washington where it wasn't yet lunchtime.

Needing to discuss another case with the commissioner of the Police Judiciaire, Maigret left his office, papers in hand. As he crossed the waiting room he sensed a presence in a shadowy corner. He turned and was surprised to see Lognon in one of the chairs, who gave him a wan smile.

It was almost six o'clock. The offices were starting to empty out, and the broad, still dusty corridor was deserted.

Normally, if Lognon needed to talk to him, he would have telephoned or, if he was in the neighbourhood, got the office boy to say he was waiting. He could even have gone into the inspectors' office because he was pretty much part of the team, even if he didn't work at the Quai.

But oh no! He had erred, so now he felt the need to be humbler than humble, to sit there like some poor wretch who waits around until someone is kind enough to favour him with a fleeting glance.

Maigret almost lost his temper because he sensed that this show of humility was another form of pride. The message seemed to be:

'You see! I proved myself unworthy. You could have had me up before the disciplinary board, but you were kind to me. I acknowledge that and I'm putting myself in my rightful place, that of a poor devil who asks for charity.'

So idiotic! It was pure Lognon, and it was probably this aspect of his character that made trying to help him such a disheartening exercise. He was even treating his cold as some sort of penance!

27

He had gone home to get changed. His suit was just as drab as the one he had been wearing that morning, and his shoes were already sopping wet. As for overcoats, he must have only one of those in his wardrobe.

If he had done his shopping in Paris, he had definitely taken buses, waiting for them on street corners in the pouring rain *on purpose*.

'*I* don't have a car to run around in! I can't take taxis, I don't want to either, because at the end of the month it's beneath my dignity to argue with the cashier, who always seems to accuse people of cheating on their expenses. I don't cheat on anything. I am an honest man, a scrupulous man.'

Maigret called to him:

'Do you want to talk to me?'

'I've got plenty of time. Whenever you've got a moment.'

'Go and wait for me in my office, then.'

'I'll wait here.'

Fool! Lugubrious fool! Still, you couldn't help pitying him. He was obviously very unhappy. He was worrying himself sick.

Maigret left the commissioner's office twenty minutes later, and Lognon hadn't moved, hadn't smoked. He had just stayed there, rooted to the spot in the waiting room, dripping like an umbrella.

'Come in. Sit down.'

'I thought I should probably bring you up to date with what I've found out. You didn't give me any specific instructions at lunchtime, so I gathered that I should just do my best.'

Still that display of excessive humility. Yet in Lognon's case it was usually an excess of arrogance that made him so unbearable.

'I went back to the Hôtel Wagram, where Bill Larner still hasn't shown his face, and I got some information about him.'

'So did I,' Maigret almost said.

But what was the point?

'He's had the same room for almost two years. I had a look. His luggage is still there. He seems only to have taken a briefcase with his papers, because I couldn't find any letters or a passport in his drawers. His clothes come from the best tailors. He lives on a grand scale, tipping lavishly and regularly entertaining women, always the same kind, the kind you meet in nightclubs. According to the concierge, he only likes brunettes, on the small side but curvy.'

Lognon very nearly blushed.

'I asked if any male friends came to see him. Apparently not. He did, however, get a lot of telephone calls. No post. Ever. One of the receptionists thought that he often ate at a restaurant on Rue des Acacias, Chez Pozzo, which he saw him go into several times.'

'Have you been to Chez Pozzo?'

'Not yet. I thought you would prefer to go there yourself. I questioned the staff of the post office on Avenue Niel. That's where Larner had his mail sent to a poste restante address. Mainly letters from the United States. He picked up his post yesterday morning. They haven't seen him today, but there's nothing for him.'

'Is that all?'

'Almost. I went to the Préfecture and at immigration I found his file because he regularly renewed his residents' card. He was born in Omaha – I don't know where that is, but it's in America – and he is forty-five.'

Lognon produced from his wallet one of those passport-size photographs of which foreigners have to submit multiple copies when they apply for their card. If the photo was to be believed, Bill Larner was a good-looking man with a knowing glint in his eye; a bon vivant, who was just starting to put on a little weight.

'I haven't found out anything else. I searched my apartment for fingerprints but they didn't leave any. They used a master key to get in.'

'Is your wife better?'

'She had an attack soon after I got there. She is in bed.'

Why couldn't he say this in a more normal voice? He seemed to be apologizing for his wife's health, as if it was his personal responsibility, and the whole world was blaming him for it.

'I almost forgot. I stopped at the garage at Porte Maillot to show them the photo. It was definitely Larner who hired the car. When he paid the deposit, he took a wad of notes out of his trouser pocket. Apparently it was all thousand-franc notes. As the car was right there, I looked it over. They had cleaned it, but you could still see stains on the back seat which were probably bloodstains.'

'No bullet holes?'

'I didn't find any.'

He blew his nose the way some women who are having a hard time suddenly shed a tear or two as they're talking.

'What do you plan on doing now?' Maigret asked, trying not to look at him.

The sight of Lognon's red nose and watery eyes was making Maigret's eyelids sting, and he thought he was catching his cold. Still, he couldn't help pitying him. In a matter of hours, the inspector had slogged from one end of Paris to the other in the cold rain. A few telephone calls would have achieved pretty much the same results, but what was the point of telling him? Didn't he need to punish himself?

'I'll do whatever you tell me to do. I am grateful to you for letting me be a part of this investigation, because I have no right to be.'

'Is your wife waiting for you to get back for dinner?'

'She never waits for me. Even if she were waiting for me . . .'

You felt like shouting: 'Enough! Be a man, for heaven's sake!'

But instead, as if involuntarily, Maigret gave him a sort of present.

'Listen, Lognon. It's now six thirty. I am going to telephone my wife to say I'm not coming home, and you and I are going to have dinner together at Pozzo's. Maybe we'll find out something.'

He went next door to brief Janvier, who was on duty, then put on his heavy overcoat, and within minutes they were waiting for a taxi on the corner of the embankment. It was still raining. Paris was like a train tunnel; the lights looked unnatural, people hugged the walls as if they were fleeing some mysterious threat.

Maigret had a thought on the way and told the car to stop outside a bistro.

'I need to make a call. We can have a quick aperitif.'

'Do you need me?'

'No. Why?'

'I'd rather wait in the car. I get heartburn if I drink.'

It was a little bar frequented mostly by taxi drivers, very hot, very smoky and with the telephone by the kitchen.

'Immigration? Is that you, Robin? Evening, my friend. Do you mind seeing if the two names I'm about to tell you are in your records?'

He spelled out Cinaglia and Cicero's names.

'I just need to know if they've been given residence permits.'

No mention of them. The two men hadn't been near the Préfecture, which suggested they weren't planning on staying in Paris long.

'Rue des Acacias.'

It seemed as if today was his day to be in a generous mood. He brought Lognon up to date in the taxi.

'The two dark-haired characters who went to Place Constantin-Pecqueur on Tuesday seem to be Charlie Cinaglia and Cicero. They are obviously partners of Larner. He got them the car, and it was Larner who went to your apartment the second time. Probably because they don't speak French.'

'I thought of that too.'

'The first time they weren't looking for papers but for someone, living or dead, the man they'd thrown out on to the pavement in Rue Fléchier. That's why they looked under the bed and in the cupboards. When they didn't find anything, they wanted to know who you were and where they could find you, so they sent Larner, who searched the sideboard.'

'They know I'm in the police now.'

'That must bother them. The newspapers' silence probably worries them too.'

'Aren't you afraid they'll leave Paris?'

'To be on the safe side, I've alerted all the stations, airports and traffic police. I've circulated their descriptions, or rather, Janvier's seeing to it as we speak.'

Even in the shadowy taxi, he could make out Lognon's faint smile.

'And that's why there's all this talk of the great Maigret! Whereas a lowly inspector like me conducts his investigations by pounding the streets, the famous chief inspector only has to telephone Washington, give orders to a swarm of assistants and put the stations and gendarmeries on alert!'

Good old Lognon! Maigret wanted to give him a slap on the knee and say, 'Come on, no need to pretend!'

Maybe deep down Lognon would have regretted forfeiting the title of Inspector Hard-Done-By. He needed to moan and groan, needed to feel he was the unluckiest man on earth.

The taxi stopped in the narrow Rue des Acacias, opposite a restaurant with red-and-white-checked curtains at its window and door. As soon as he stepped inside, Maigret was hit by a blast of the New York he had got to know with Jimmy MacDonald. Pozzo's didn't look like a Parisian restaurant, but one of the sort you find in practically every street off Broadway. The lighting was very soft and took a while to get used to. At first you could barely make out anything, and faces hung blurrily in a kind of half-light.

There was a row of high stools along the mahogany bar, and little American, Italian and French flags were dotted between the bottles on the shelves. A radio or gramophone was playing quietly. Nine or ten tables were laid with tablecloths in the same checks as the curtains, and the panelled walls were hung with photographs of boxers and show-business personalities – especially boxers – most of which were signed.

At that time of day the room was almost empty. Two men were playing poker dice with the barman at the bar. A couple at the back were eating spaghetti under the dreamy gaze of a waiter who stood by the hatch leading to the kitchen.

No one hurried forward to greet them. All eyes merely turned for a moment towards the strange pair that Maigret and the skinny, lugubrious Lognon made. There was a special sort of silence, as if someone had called out just as they were opening the door, 'Look out! Cops!'

Maigret thought about sitting at the bar, then chose the table closest to it after taking off his coat and hat. There was a delicious smell of spicy food, with a strong tinge of garlic. The dice started rolling on the bar again, but the barman continued observing his new customers with a wryly amused expression.

The waiter wordlessly handed them a menu.

'Do you like spaghetti, Lognon?'

'I'll have whatever you're having.'

'Well then, two spaghettis to start.'

'To drink?'

'A bottle of chianti.'

He let his gaze wander over the photographs, then stood up and went over to examine one more closely. It must have been taken quite a while ago. It was of a stocky young boxer and signed, with a dedication to Pozzo: Charlie Cinaglia.

The man at the bar still hadn't taken his eyes off him. Without stopping playing, he called out from a distance:

'Interested in boxing, eh?'

Maigret replied:

'Maybe in certain boxers. Are you Pozzo?'

'I suppose you're Maigret?'

It was a mild, easy-going exchange, like two tennis players knocking up before a match.

When the waiter put the bottle of chianti on the table, Pozzo continued:

'I thought you only drank beer.'

He was small and bald, apart from a few strands of very dark hair combed over the top of his skull. He had big, round eyes, a nose as bulbous as Lognon's and a wide, rubbery clown's mouth. He spoke Italian to the two men sitting across the bar from him. They were both dressed with extremely studied elegance; no doubt Maigret would have found their names in his files. The younger one clearly took drugs.

'Help yourself, Lognon.'

'After you, sir.'

Perhaps Lognon had really never had spaghetti. Or was he doing it on purpose? He dutifully imitated Maigret's every move, like a guest straining with all his might to please his host.

'Don't you like it?'

'It's not bad at all.'

'Do you want me to order something else?'

'Not on your life! I'm sure this is very good for you.'

The spaghetti kept slipping off his fork, and the young woman eating at the back of the restaurant couldn't help bursting out laughing. At the bar the game of poker dice came to an end. The two customers shook hands with Pozzo, glanced at Maigret, then strolled slowly to the exit, as if they wanted to show that they had nothing to fear, nothing on their consciences.

'Pozzo!'

'Yes, inspector . . .'

The Italian was even smaller than he looked behind his bar. His legs were especially short, which was emphasized by the pair of very baggy trousers he was wearing.

He walked over to the policemen's table wearing a fake smile, with a white napkin over his arm.

'So, you like Italian food, do you?'

Rather than answer, Maigret glanced at the photograph of the boxer.

'Has it been long since you've seen Charlie?'

'You know Charlie? So you've been to America, then?'

'Have you?'

'Me? I lived there for twenty years.'

'In St Louis?'

'In Chicago, St Louis, Brooklyn.'

'When did Charlie come in with Bill Larner?'

Maigret was increasingly reminded of his stay in the United States. He sensed Lognon was listening to their conversation with amazement.

It was true, it wasn't going the way such things normally did in France. Pozzo wasn't behaving the way owners of shady restaurants usually do when they are questioned by the police.

Instead he was standing over them, affable, relaxed, an ironic glint in his big eyes. Pouting comically, he scratched his head.

'So you know Bill too! Sweet Bill, eh? A very likeable guy.'

'He's a good customer of yours, isn't he?'

'Would you say?'

He sat down unapologetically at their table.

'A glass, Angelino.'

He poured himself some chianti.

'Don't worry. The bottle's on me. Dinner too. It's not every day that I have the honour of playing host to Detective Chief Inspector Maigret.'

'Are you enjoying yourself, Pozzo?'

'I always enjoy myself. Not like your friend. Has he lost his wife?'

He studied Lognon with an air of mock commiseration.

'Angelino! Bring these gentlemen *scaloppine alla Fiorentina*. Tell Giovanni to prepare them as he would for me. Do you like escalopes done the Florentine way, inspector?'

'I met Charlie Cinaglia three days ago.'

'Did you just fly in from New York?'

'Charlie was in Paris.'

'Really? You see what these people are like. Ten years ago, it was good old Pozzo this, good old Pozzo that. I think he even called me Papa Pozzo. Now he's in Paris and he doesn't even come and see me!'

'Same with Bill Larner? And Tony Cicero?'

'What was that last name you said?'

He wasn't trying to hide the fact that he was putting on an act. Quite the opposite. He was playing it up on purpose, more and more like a clown performing his routine. But when you looked at him closely, you noticed that, for all his face-pulling and wisecracking, his eyes remained hard and watchful.

'It's funny. I knew a lot of Tonys but I don't remember a Cicero.'

'From St Louis.'

'You went to St Louis? That's where I became an American citizen. Which I am, by the way.'

'But you're living in France now. And the French government could very easily revoke your licence.'

'What for? Doesn't my place comply with hygiene regulations? Ask at the local police station. We never get any fights. Never any soliciting either. In fact, the chief inspector, who I'm sure you know, is good enough to come and have dinner here with his wife from time to time. It's not that busy now. Our clientele get here later. Let me know what you think of these *scaloppine*.'

'Do you have a telephone?'

'Of course. The booth is at the back, on the left, the door next to the bathrooms.'

Maigret got up and ensconced himself in the booth. He dialled the number of the Police Judiciaire, spoke almost under his breath.

'Janvier? I'm at Chez Pozzo, the restaurant on Rue des Acacias. Tell surveillance to put a tap on this line all evening. You've got time. It won't be for half an hour. Tell them to make a note of all the conversations, especially if any of the three following names are mentioned.'

He spelled out Cinaglia, Cicero and Bill Larner's names.

'Any news?'

'No. We're going through Hotel Agency files.'

When he went back into the room, he found Pozzo trying unsuccessfully to get a smile out of Lognon.

'So you didn't come and see me for my cooking?'

'Listen, Pozzo. Charlie and Cicero have been in Paris for a fortnight, you know that as well as I do. They probably met Larner here.'

'I don't know Cicero but, as far as Charlie is concerned, he must have changed a lot because I didn't recognize him.'

'That'll do! For certain reasons I want to have a private conversation with these gentlemen.'

'All three of them?'

'It's a serious business, a murder.'

Pozzo crossed himself jokily.

'Do you understand? We're not in America, where it's hard work proving pretty much anything.'

'You're hurting my feelings, inspector. Really, I wasn't expecting this from you.'

Then, holding up his glass, he said:

'Cheers! And there I was, so happy to meet you! I'd heard all about you, like everybody. I thought to myself: "Now, there's a man who knows about life." Then you come and see me and treat me as if it was news to you that Pozzo has never harmed a soul. You go on about some little boxer who I haven't seen for ten or fifteen years, insinuating something or other.'

'Enough! I'm not having an argument today. I've warned you. I've said we're dealing with a murder.'

'Strange I haven't read anything about it in the papers. Who was killed?'

'Doesn't matter. If Charlie and Cicero have been here, if you have the slightest idea of where they are, I'll see you're charged with complicity.'

Pozzo shook his head sadly.

'You'd do that to me.'

'Have they been here?'

'When are you claiming they walked through my door?'

'Have they been here?'

'We get so many people passing through! At times all the tables are full, and there are people queuing out into the street. I can't see everything that goes on.'

'Have they been here?'

'Listen. We're going to make a deal, and you'll see that Pozzo can be a real friend. I promise that if they set foot in here I will telephone you immediately. Is that on the level, eh? Tell me what this Cicero looks like.'

'There's no point.'

'So how do you expect me to recognize him? Am I meant to ask my customers for their passports? Is that what I'm meant to do? I'm married; I've got a family. I have always respected the laws of whatever country I'm in. I might as well tell you: I've applied for French citizenship.'

'After being granted American citizenship?'

'That was a mistake. I don't like the climate over there. I'm sure your friend will understand.'

He gave Lognon a bitterly ironic look, and Lognon blew his nose for a long time, not knowing where to turn.

'Waiter!' called Maigret.

'I've already told you that you're my guest.'

'I'm sorry but I can't accept.'

'I'd take that as an insult.'

'That's your choice. Waiter! Bring me the bill.'

Maigret was not really as angry as he seemed. Pozzo was a tough customer, but he didn't mind that. Nor did he mind dealing with characters who had got the better of the American police. Genuine hard men who played for keeps. MacDonald had said Cinaglia was a killer, hadn't he? It would be quite enjoyable telephoning Washington in a few days and casually saying, 'Hello, Jimmy! . . . I've got them.'

Maigret hadn't the slightest idea of the identity of the man who had been tipped out on to the pavement on Rue

Fléchier, almost at Inspector Lognon's feet. He didn't even know if the stranger was dead or not.

As for the second car, which had taken charge of the corpse, or wounded man, or whatever it was, that was even more of a blank.

As far as he could tell, two groups were involved. The first comprised, at the very least, Charlie Cinaglia, Tony Cicero and Larner, who had hired the car and searched Lognon's papers.

But who was in the second car? Why had they run the risk of picking up a body from the pavement?

If the man was dead, what had they done with the body?

And if he wasn't, where was he being looked after?

This was one of the rare investigations where they were starting out without any leads. These people had apparently crossed the Atlantic to settle scores of which the French police were entirely ignorant.

The only reference point for the moment was Pozzo's bar and restaurant, with its New York ambience weirdly transplanted to within a few metres of the Arc de Triomphe.

'I hope I'll be able to return the favour one day,' muttered the Italian as Maigret got up after paying.

'What do you mean?'

'I mean, inspector, that I am sure that one day you will allow me to give you a good dinner without insulting me by bringing out your wallet.'

His broad mouth was smiling, but his eyes weren't. He saw the two men to the door, taking a malicious delight in giving Lognon a friendly slap on the shoulder.

'Shall I call you a taxi?'

'No need for that.'

'It's true it's not raining any more. Well then, good evening, detective chief inspector. I hope this gentleman will get over the loss of his wife.'

The door finally closed behind them, and the two policemen set off along the pavement. Lognon didn't say anything. Perhaps, deep down, he enjoyed seeing Maigret being treated like a novice.

'I've had their telephone tapped,' Maigret said, when they were almost at the corner of the street.

'I thought you might.'

Maigret frowned. If Lognon had suspected as much when he saw him heading to the telephone booth, how much more likely was a man like Pozzo to have done so too?

'In that case he won't telephone. He's more likely to send a message.'

The street was deserted. A garage across the road was closed. Avenue MacMahon was still glistening with rain, and only a taxi cruising for fares and two or three silhouettes over by Grande-Armée were to be seen.

'I think you'd better keep an eye on the place, Lognon. You haven't slept much recently, so I'll send someone to relieve you in a moment.'

'I'm on night duty all this week.'

'But you're meant to have a sleep during the day and you haven't.'

'It doesn't matter.'

Still as infuriating as ever! Maigret had to draw on reserves of patience with him that he would never have shown to Janvier or Lucas or any of his inspectors.

'As soon as he gets here, go home to bed.'

'If that's an order . . .'

'It is. If you have to leave before that, do your best to call headquarters.'

'Right, sir.'

Maigret left him on the corner of the street, then walked quickly to Avenue des Ternes, where he went into a bar and asked for a token.

'Janvier? Any news from the phone tap? Fine. Who have you got with you? Torrence? Tell him to jump in a taxi and go to Rue des Acacias. He'll find Lognon there on a stakeout. Tell him to relieve him. Lognon will fill him in.'

He took a taxi home and had a small glass of sloe gin and chatted with his wife.

'Madame Lognon telephoned.'

'What about?'

'She hasn't heard from her husband since the start of the afternoon and she's worried. Apparently he looked under the weather.'

He shrugged and was about to telephone her . . . Oh come on! Enough was enough. He went to bed, slept and was woken by the smell of coffee. As he got dressed, he couldn't help thinking of Lognon.

When he got to Quai des Orfèvres at nine, Lucas had taken over from Janvier, who had gone home to bed.

'No news from Torrence?'

'He telephoned yesterday evening, around ten. Apparently he didn't find Lognon in Rue des Acacias.'

'Where is he?'

'Torrence? Still over there. He just called again to ask if he should carry on watching the place. I told him to ring back in a few minutes.'

Maigret asked for the number of the Lognons' apartment.

'This is Detective Chief Inspector Maigret.'

'Do you have any news of my husband? I haven't slept all night . . .'

'Isn't he at home?'

'What? You don't know where he is?'

'You don't either?'

It was absurd. Now he had to reassure her, tell her some story or other.

Between Maigret leaving him on the corner of Rue des Acacias and Torrence arriving to replace him, Lognon had disappeared.

He hadn't telephoned, hadn't given any sign of life.

'Admit it, you think, like me, that something has happened to him . . . I always knew it would end like this . . . And here I am, infirm and all on my own up here on this fifth floor, which I can't even leave!'

Goodness only knows what he said to calm her down. He felt nauseated by the time he had finished.

3.

Maigret was waiting in a furious mood, his hands in his overcoat pockets, stamping his feet and trying to peer over the checked curtains to see what was happening at the back of the restaurant. When he had got to Rue des Acacias he had been surprised not to find Pozzo's door open. There was a light on inside, though, a single bulb burning at the back of the restaurant.

He had knocked on the window two or three times and had the impression someone was moving. There was no rain this morning, but it was so cold that it felt as if it was going to freeze, and the sky was the colour of a tin roof. The world seemed a hard, cruel place.

'He's in there, but I'd be amazed if he opened up for you,' said the grocer next door. 'This is when he does his cleaning, and he doesn't like to be disturbed. He'll only open around eleven, unless you know how to knock.'

Maigret tried again, standing on tiptoe so that part of his face could be seen over the curtain. He looked severe this morning. He didn't like anyone touching his men, even if it was just an inspector from the ninth arrondissement, and his name was Lognon.

What looked like a bear's silhouette from a distance finally started moving in the gloom, gradually becoming clearer as it approached the door, and Maigret soon made out Pozzo's face, centimetres away from his, on the other side of the glass. Only then did the Italian unhook a chain, turn a key and pull the door towards him.

'Come in,' he said, as if he were expecting Maigret's visit.

He was wearing old, saggy trousers, a pale-blue shirt with the sleeves rolled up and a pair of red slippers which made him shuffle along. Seemingly indifferent to Maigret's presence, he headed to the back of the room, where a solitary light was on, and sat back down in his chair, in front of the remains of a substantial breakfast.

'Make yourself comfortable. Do you want a cup of coffee?'

'No.'

'A quick drink?'

'No.'

Without a flicker of surprise, Pozzo gave a nod as if to say, 'Fine. No hard feelings.'

He was a little grey in the face, and there were rings under his eyes. Actually, he looked less like a clown now than one of those old comic actors whose faces have become rubbery from all their contortions. Those veterans who have been everywhere and seen everything and acquired that same world-weary look.

In a corner, brooms and a bucket were up against the wall. Through the hatch he could see the kitchen, from which came a smell of bacon.

'I thought you were married and had children.'

As if he were acting a scene in slow motion, Pozzo scratched his head, went to get a cigar from a box on a shelf, lit it, then blew the smoke almost directly into Maigret's face.

'Does your wife live at Quai des Orfèvres?' he said finally.

'Don't you live here?'

'I could tell you that's none of your business. I could even show you the door, and you'd still have no grounds for complaint. Do we understand each other? Yesterday I welcomed you with open arms and tried to give you dinner on the house. Not because I like cops – I mean no offence by that either – but because you are someone in your field, and I respect people who make a name for themselves in their line of work. But fine! You didn't want to be my guest. That's your business. Now you show up again this morning and disturb me to ask questions. It's up to me whether I answer or not.'

'Would you rather I took you to the Police Judiciaire?'

'Now, that's another story, and I would be curious to see what happened. You're forgetting that I am still an American citizen. Before I came along, I'd be sure to telephone my consul.'

He had sat down in front of his empty plate, resting an elbow on the table like someone who feels at home, and was observing Maigret through the smoke of his cigar.

'You see, Monsieur Maigret, you've been spoiled. Someone reminded me yesterday evening, after you'd left, that you'd been to America. I found that rather hard to believe. I wonder what your colleagues over there showed you exactly. They must have told you that it's not the same as here, though. Imagine I'm at home. Do you understand that concept? Suppose someone comes into your apartment and starts asking your wife questions . . . But fine! I'm only saying that so you know who you're dealing with, and, most of all, so you know that if I listen to you and answer your questions, it's because I want to. So there's no point threatening me, like you did last night, with withdrawing my licence. Now to get back to your question: I have no reason to conceal from you the fact that my wife and my children live in the country, because this is no place for them, or that I sleep most nights in a room on the mezzanine, or, last of all, that I do the cleaning round here in the morning.'

'How did you warn Charlie and Larner?'

'I'm sorry?'

'Yesterday, after I left, you told Charlie and his friends about my visit.'

'Really?'

'You didn't telephone them.'

'Presumably my telephone is tapped?'

'Where is Charlie?'

Pozzo sighed and looked over at the photograph of Cinaglia in his boxing days.

'Yesterday,' Maigret went on, 'I warned you that this was a serious business. It's even more so this morning, because the inspector who was with me has disappeared.'

'The cheerful one?'

'When we came out of here I left him at the corner of the street. Half an hour later he wasn't there any more and he hasn't been seen since. Do you understand what that means?'

'Am I supposed to?'

Maigret managed to keep calm, but his resolve had hardened too, and he looked Pozzo unwaveringly in the eye.

'I want to know how you warned them. I want to know where they're hiding. Bill Larner hasn't been back to the Hôtel Wagram. The other two have gone to ground somewhere, very likely in Paris, and more than likely not far from here, since you were able to get them a message in a few minutes without using your telephone. You'd better come clean, Pozzo. When does the waiter get here?'

'Midday.'

'And the chef?'

'Three. We don't do lunch.'

'They'll both be questioned.'

'That's your business, isn't it?'

'Where's Charlie?'

Pozzo, who looked as if he was thinking, slowly got to his feet. With what seemed like a reluctant sigh, he went over to the photograph of the boxer and examined it attentively.

'On your trip to the United States, did you go to Chicago, or Detroit, or St Louis?'

'I travelled all over the Midwest.'

'You probably noticed that those guys aren't choirboys, eh? Was it before or after Prohibition?'

'After.'

'Right. Well, during Prohibition it was maybe five or even ten times tougher.'

Maigret waited, not knowing what he was driving at.

'I worked for five years as a maître d' in Chicago before setting up on my own in St Louis. I opened a restaurant like this one, which attracted people of all sorts: politicians, boxers, gangsters and entertainers. Well, Monsieur Maigret, I never fell out with anyone, not even with the lieutenant of police who'd come and have a double whiskey at my bar every now and then. And do you know why?'

He was drawing it out, like an old ham.

'Because I never got involved in other people's business. What makes you think I'd change my principles when I got to Paris? Wasn't your spaghetti good? That's something I'm ready to discuss with you.'

'But you refuse to tell me where Charlie is?'

'Listen, Maigret . . .'

He might just as easily have called him Jules. He stopped just short of adopting a paternal tone and putting a hand on his shoulder.

'In Paris, you're something of a big shot, and people say you almost always come out on top. Do you want me to tell you why that is?'

'What I want is Charlie's address.'

'Let's not talk about that. We are dealing with serious matters now. You win because you're only ever up against amateurs. There aren't any amateurs over there. Even with the third degree, it is very rare they get someone who is determined to hold his tongue to talk.'

'Charlie is a killer.'

'Is he now? I suppose the FBI told you that, did they? Did the FBI also tell you why, in that case, Charlie hasn't been sent to the electric chair yet?'

Maigret had decided to let him keep talking. He stopped listening once or twice and looked around, frowning, as he pursued his train of thought. Charlie and his companions had clearly been told of his and Lognon's visit to Rue des Acacias. It hadn't been done by telephone. If someone had left the restaurant to warn them, he or she couldn't have had to go far. And Lognon would have been suspicious if he had seen the waiter, say, or the cook, or Pozzo himself leave the restaurant.

'That's the difference, Maigret, the whole difference between amateurs and professionals. Didn't I tell you just now that I respect people who are someone in their field?'

'Including killers?'

'You told me a story yesterday. It has nothing to do with me, and I've already forgotten it. Now you're back with another instalment, and I'm not interested. You are a good man, probably an honourable one too. You have a fine reputation. I don't know if those gentlemen from the FBI asked you to deal with this business, but I doubt it. So now I'm telling you: 'Drop it!''

'Thank you for the advice.'

'It's sincere. When Charlie boxed in Chicago, he was a featherweight, and it never crossed his mind to go up against a heavyweight.'

'When did you see him again?'

Pozzo remained almost ostentatiously silent.

'I suppose you can't tell me the name of the two customers who you were playing poker dice with yesterday either?'

A look of astonishment crossed Pozzo's face.

'Am I meant to know my customers' names, addresses and marital statuses?'

Maigret had got to his feet as Pozzo had done earlier and, with the same distracted air, gone over to the bar. He went round behind it and bent down to the shelves under the counter.

Pozzo followed him with his eyes, apparently indifferent.

'You see, when I find one of those customers, I've a feeling that things will start to go badly for you.'

Maigret held up a notepad and pencil he had just found.

'Now I know how you warned Charlie, or Bill Larner, or Cicero – it doesn't matter which, as they're working together. My mistake was to think you did it after I left. But it was before. When you saw the inspector and me come in, you knew what it was about. You had time while we ordered to scribble a few words on the pad and pass the note to one of the two customers. What do you say to that?'

'I say it's very interesting.'

'Is that all?'

'That's all.'

The telephone rang in the booth. Frowning, Pozzo went to answer it.

'It's for you!' he announced.

It was the Police Judiciaire, Maigret having said where he would be when he left. Lucas was on the other end of the line.

'We've found him, chief.'

Something in Lucas' voice suggested that events had taken an unpleasant turn.

'Dead?'

'No. About an hour ago, a fish wholesaler from Honfleur driving along the Nationale 13 in his van picked up a man lying unconscious by the side of the road between Poissy and Le Pecq, in the Saint-Germain forest.'

'Lognon?'

'Yes. Apparently he's in a bad way. The wholesaler took him to a Doctor Grenier, in Saint-Germain, and the doctor has just telephoned.'

'Is he injured?'

'His face is swollen, probably from being punched, but it is the head wound that is the most serious. According to the doctor, he's apparently been badly pistol-whipped. As a precaution I've asked for him to be taken straight to Beaujon by ambulance. He'll be there in three-quarters of an hour.'

'Anything else?'

'The Hotel Agency have picked up the two men's trail.'

'Charlie and Cicero?'

'Yes. Ten days ago, when they came in from Le Havre, they stayed at the Hôtel de l'Étoile in Rue Brey. They were out last Monday night. On Tuesday morning they came to pay their bill and pick up their luggage.'

It all revolved around the same part of town: Rue Brey, the Hôtel Wagram, Pozzo's restaurant, Rue des Acacias, the garage where the car had been hired.

'Is that all?'

'A car that had been stolen from Avenue de la Grande-Armée yesterday evening at around nine was found this morning at Porte Maillot. It belongs to an engineer who was playing bridge at a friend's house. He says the car had been cleaned yesterday afternoon. When it was found it was covered with mud, as if it had been driven on country lanes.'

Always the same part of town.

'What do I do, chief?'

'Go to Beaujon and wait for me.'

'Shall I tell Madame Lognon?'

Maigret heaved a sigh.

'That would be best, of course. Don't go into details. Tell her he's not dead. Best not do it over the telephone. You could stop off at Place Constantin-Pecqueur before going to Beaujon.'

'That'll be fun.'

'Just say there was a fist fight.'

'OK.'

Maigret almost smiled. For once the lugubrious Lognon actually seemed to have luck on his side. If he was seriously wounded, he was going to become a sort of hero, probably get a medal!

'See you soon, chief.'

'See you then.'

While he was on the telephone, Pozzo had stacked the chairs on the tables and was now sweeping his restaurant.

'My inspector has been given a beating,' Maigret said, looking him in the eye.

No reaction.

'Just a beating?'

'Are you surprised?'

'Not particularly. It's probably a warning. That happens a lot over there.'

'Still determined to keep your trap shut?'

'I told you that I never get involved in other people's business.'

'We'll be seeing each other.'

'It will be a pleasure.'

As he was leaving, Maigret turned and went and picked up the notepad he had left on a table. Finally he glimpsed a hint of anxiety on the restaurateur's face.

'Wait a minute! That's mine.'

'I'll give it back to you.'

He found the car from the Préfecture waiting for him outside.

'Beaujon.'

In Faubourg Saint-Honoré, at the dark hospital gates, he gave the notepad to the policeman who was driving.

'Go back to Quai des Orfèvres. Go up to the laboratory and give this to Moers. Handle it with care.'

'What shall I tell him?'

'Nothing. He'll know what it's about.'

Confident that he still had plenty of time before the ambulance got there, he went into a bistro, ordered a calvados and shut himself away in the telephone booth.

'Moers? Maigret here. A notepad is on its way to you from me. There's a good chance someone wrote a few words in pencil on it yesterday evening, then tore out the page.'

'Understood. You want to know if it left an impression on the page below?'

'Exactly. The pad may not have been used since, but I can't say for certain. Be quick about it. I'll be at the office around noon.'

'All right, chief.'

When it came down to it, Maigret couldn't help but be affected by Pozzo's self-assurance. There was a grain of truth, more in fact, in what the restaurateur had said. You often heard people at the Police Judiciaire saying that most, if not all, murderers were idiots.

'Amateurs!' Pozzo had claimed.

He wasn't entirely wrong. On this side of the Atlantic ten per cent, at most, of all murderers eluded the police, whereas over there known killers like Cinaglia were free to go where they pleased, because nothing could be proved against them.

They were professionals who, to use another of Pozzo's idioms, played hardball. Maigret couldn't remember anyone ever saying, 'Drop it!' in that fatherly way before.

Of course he had no intention of doing so, but he couldn't help thinking that MacDonald hadn't been exactly encouraging on the telephone yesterday.

He was in unfamiliar territory. He was up against people whose methods he only knew by hearsay and whose ways of thinking and reacting were new to him.

Why had Charlie and Tony Cicero come to Paris? They seemed to have crossed the ocean with a specific end in mind and not wasted any time.

Eight days after they got here they were dumping a body on the pavement by Notre-Dame-de-Lorette church.

That body, whether dead or alive, had disappeared a few minutes later, almost before Lognon's very eyes.

'Same again!'

He knocked back a second calvados, feeling as if he were coming down with a cold, then crossed the street and went under the arch as an ambulance was pulling in.

It was Lognon, whom they had brought from Saint-Germain and who was insisting on walking. When he saw Maigret, they could no longer keep him on the stretcher.

'I'm telling you I can still stand.'

Maigret had to look away for a moment. Despite everything he couldn't help smiling when he saw Inspector Hard-Done-By's face. One eye was swollen and completely closed, and the Saint-Germain doctor had covered one of his nostrils and the corner of his mouth with a shocking pink plaster.

'I must explain, sir . . .'

'In a minute.'

Poor Lognon was unsteady on his feet, and a nurse had to support him as he was steered to the room that had been got ready for him. The house doctor went in after him.

'Call me when you've seen to him. Make sure that he can talk.'

Maigret paced up and down the corridor, where he was joined ten minutes later by Lucas.

'How was Madame Lognon? Was it hard?'

Lucas' look was eloquent.

'She is outraged that he hasn't been taken home. She says we have no right to keep him in hospital and keep the two of them apart like this.'

'How does she propose to look after him?'

'I pointed that out to her. She wants to see you and is talking about going to the prefect of police. According to her, we are leaving her on her own, sick and unprotected, at the mercy of gangsters.'

'Did you tell her their building was being watched?'

'Yes. That calmed her down a little. I had to take her over to the window and show her the man on duty outside.'

'It's always the same, some people get all the credit while others do all the dirty work!' she said finally.

When the house doctor came out of the room, he was worried.

'Fracture of the skull?' Maigret asked in a low voice.

'I don't think so. We're going to x-ray him in a moment, but it's unlikely. But he was knocked out. What's more, he has been out in the woods all night and he may have got pneumonia. You can talk to him. That will make him feel better. He's asking for you, won't let us do anything to him until he's seen you. I had a terrible job giving him a penicillin injection. I had to show him the name of the

59

medicine on the phial because he was afraid I was trying to put him to sleep.'

'Better if I see him alone,' Maigret said to Lucas.

Lognon was lying in a white bed, while a nurse bustled around the room. His face was burning hot now, as if the fever was building.

Maigret sat down by his bed.

'Well, my friend?'

'They got me.'

A tear spurted from his uncovered eye.

'The doctor says you shouldn't get worked up. Just give me the essentials.'

'When you left me, I stayed at the corner, where I could watch the door of the restaurant. I was standing right by the wall, some way away from the streetlight.'

'Did anyone leave Pozzo's?'

'No, no one. After about ten minutes a car came down Avenue MacMahon, turned the corner and stopped directly in front of me.'

'Charlie Cinaglia?'

'There were three of them. The tall one, Cicero, was doing the driving, with Bill Larner next to him. Charlie was in the back. I didn't have time to take my gun out of my pocket. Charlie had already opened the door and was pointing his automatic at me. He didn't say anything, just signalled for me to get in. The other two didn't even look at me. What was I supposed to do?'

'Get in,' sighed Maigret.

'The car drove off immediately while I was being frisked, and my gun was taken away. No one spoke. I saw we were leaving Paris by Porte Maillot, then I recognized the Saint-Germain road.'

'Did the car stop in the forest?'

'Yes. Larner gestured to his companion which road to take. We turned off into a little lane and when we were a long way from the main road, the car pulled up. Then they made me get out.'

Pozzo had been right to say they weren't amateurs.

'Charlie kept his mouth shut virtually the whole time. It was the tall one, Cicero, who stood there with his hands in his pockets, chain-smoking, telling Larner in English what to ask me.'

'So they'd taken Larner along as an interpreter?'

'I got the feeling he wasn't that thrilled with his role in the whole thing. Several times he seemed to be telling them to let me go. Before they started questioning me, Charlie, the short one, smashed his fist into my face, and my nose started bleeding.

'"I think you'd better be nice," Larner said with a slight accent, "and tell these gentlemen what they want to know."

'They basically asked me the same question over and over, "What have you done with the body?"

'At first I didn't want to do them the honour of answering and just gave them a hard look. Then Cicero said something in English to Charlie, who punched me again.

'"You're making a mistake," said Larner with a bored expression. "You see, everyone always talks in the end."

'After the third or fourth punch, I can't remember how many now, I swore to them that I didn't know what had happened to the body, that I didn't even know whose it was. They didn't believe me. Cicero carried on smoking his cigarette and pacing up and down every now and then to stretch his legs.

'"Who told the police?"

'What was I supposed to say? That I just happened to be there on another matter that had nothing to do with them?'

'Each time I replied, Cicero signalled to Charlie, who couldn't wait to punch me in the face again. They emptied my pockets, examined the contents of my wallet in the car headlights.'

'Did it go on for long?'

'I don't know. Maybe half an hour, maybe more. I hurt all over. One of the punches had given me a black eye, and I felt the blood running down my face.

'"I swear to you," I said to them, "I don't know anything."

'Cicero wasn't satisfied and began talking to Larner again, who then started a new line of questioning. He asked me if I'd seen another car stop on Rue Fléchier. I said I had.

'"What was the licence number?"

'"I didn't have time to see it."

'"You're lying!"

'"I'm not lying."

'They wanted to know who you were, because they had seen you going into my apartment on Place Constantin-Pecqueur. I told them. Then they asked if you had been in touch with the FBI and I said that I didn't know, that in

France inspectors don't ask their superiors questions. Larner laughed. He seemed to know you.

'Eventually Cicero shrugged and headed off to the car. Larner seemed relieved and went after him, but Charlie stayed behind. He shouted something to them, from a distance. Then he took his automatic out of his pocket, and I thought he was going to kill me, I . . . .'

Lognon fell silent, tears of rage in his eyes. Maigret didn't want to know what he had done, if he had fallen to his knees, begged. Probably not. Lognon could have just stood there, sombre and bitter to the end.

'He only hit me over the head with the butt of his pistol, and I passed out. When I came to, they weren't there any more. I tried to stand up. I called for help.'

'Did you wander around in the forest all night?'

'I suppose I must have gone round in circles. I blacked out several times. Sometimes I dragged myself along with my hands. I heard cars passing, and each time I tried to shout. In the morning I found myself by the side of the road, and a van stopped.'

Without any transition, he asked, 'Does my wife know?'

'Yes. Lucas went there.'

'What did she say?'

'She insisted that you be taken back to Place Constantin-Pecqueur.'

A flash of anxiety crossed Lognon's one good eye.

'Am I going to be moved?'

'No. You need treatment and you'll be better off here.'

'I did what I could.'

'Of course you did.'

A sudden thought seemed to be worrying Lognon. He hesitated before speaking, then finally mumbled, turning his face away:

'I don't deserve to be in the police.'

'Why?'

'Because if I had known where the body was I would have ended up telling them.'

'So would I,' said Maigret, although it wasn't clear whether he was just trying to make the inspector feel better.

'Am I going to have to stay in hospital long?'

'A few days, at any rate.'

'Am I off the investigation now?'

'No, of course you'll be kept informed.'

'Do you promise? You're not angry with me?'

'About what, my friend?'

'You know very well it's my fault.'

He was really laying it on thick. Maigret had no choice but to deny it, say over and over that he had done his duty, that if he had acted differently on Monday night they might never have discovered Charlie and Cicero's trail.

Besides, it was almost true.

'What is my wife doing for shopping?'

To be on the safe side, Maigret replied, 'Lucas has taken care of it.'

'I'm ashamed to put you to all this trouble.'

Oh come on! He hadn't changed! Still humble to a fault. One way or another, he couldn't help overdoing it.

Luckily someone knocked on the door just at that moment, because Maigret didn't know how to get out of there. The nurse announced:

'It's time to go down to radiology.'

This time Lognon had to sit on a gurney, and when he passed, Lucas, who was waiting in the corridor, gave him a friendly little wave.

'Come on!'

'What did they do to him?'

Without replying directly, Maigret muttered, 'Pozzo's right. They're hard men.'

Then he said pensively:

'I'm surprised that someone like Bill Larner is working with them. Crooks of his calibre don't normally get their hands dirty.'

'Do you think the other two have forced him to help them?'

'In any case I'd like to have a chat with him.'

Larner was a professional as well, but of another kind and class, one of those international criminals who only do the occasional job, a serious, meticulously organized heist that nets them twenty or thirty thousand dollars and then they can take things easy. For the two years he had been in Paris he had apparently been able to live on his capital without any trouble.

Maigret and Lucas flagged down a taxi, and Maigret gave the Préfecture's address first. Then, as they were crossing Rue Royale, he changed his mind.

'Rue des Capucines,' he told the driver. 'The Manhattan Bar.'

The idea had come to him when he was thinking about the photographs covering Chez Pozzo's walls. The Manhattan had a similar selection of portraits of boxers and actors on its walls. Its clientele was the same as Rue des Acacias. For over twenty years Luigi had watched the American colony in Paris and the cream of the tourists visiting from the States file through his bar. It wasn't yet midday, and the place was virtually deserted. Luigi in person was behind the bar, shelving bottles.

'Good morning, detective chief inspector. What can I get you?'

He was Italian by birth, like Pozzo, and the word was that he lost more or less all his takings at the races. Not just at the races either, but on every sort of bet. Boxing matches, tennis tournaments, swimming meets – everything, even the following day's weather, was an excuse for a bet as far as he was concerned.

In the slack hours of the afternoon, between three and five, he and a friend who had some vague connection to the embassy would sometimes bet on cars in the street.

'Five thousand francs there'll be a Citroën in the next ten minutes.'

'Done!'

Maigret ordered a whiskey for local colour and let his gaze wander over the rows of photographs on the walls. He soon found Charlie Cinaglia in boxing gear. It was exactly the same photograph as at Chez Pozzo's, only this one wasn't signed.

4.

In which the implication of kindergarten persists and Maigret begins to lose his patience

When they came out of the Manhattan in matching black overcoats and hats, with Maigret looking twice as tall and bulky as Lucas, they vaguely resembled a pair of widowers who had stopped off at a string of bistros on their way back from the graveyard.

Had Luigi done it on purpose? Possibly. But if so, it hadn't been malicious. He was honest, no one ever had a bad word to say about him, and the embassy's upper echelons had no qualms about propping up his bar.

He had given them generous measures, that was all, especially Maigret, who hadn't drunk whiskey for a long time. And that was on top of the two calvados he had just had in Faubourg Saint-Honoré.

He wasn't drunk, nor was Lucas. But did Lucas think his boss was drunk? He had a strange way of glancing up at him as they threaded their way through the crowd thronging the pavements.

Lucas hadn't gone to Rue des Acacias that morning. He hadn't heard Pozzo's speech, or rather, lecture, so he couldn't really understand Maigret's frame of mind.

There had been Luigi's little lesson about boxers first – almost immediately, in fact. Maigret had looked at the photograph of Charlie and casually inquired, as if it didn't matter either way:

'Do you know him?'

'A kid who might have got the world talking about him. He was probably the best at his weight, and he had put in a lot of work to get there. Then one fine day the idiot gets mixed up in some shady scheme or other, and the Boxing Federation revokes his licence.'

'What happened to him?'

'What do you think happens to guys like that? There are thousands of kids walking into boxing gyms every year in Chicago, in Detroit, in New York, in all the big cities, thinking they're going to become champions. And how many champions do you think there are in a generation, inspector?'

'I don't know. Not many, obviously.'

'And even for them success doesn't last. The ones who haven't spent all their money on platinum blondes and Cadillacs start a restaurant or a sports shop. But what about all the others, all those kids who thought they'd made it and end up with their brains turned to mush? All they've learned to do is fight, and there'll always be people who need them, as bodyguards or muscle. That's what happened to Charlie.'

'I was told he'd become a killer.'

As if it was the most natural thing in the world, Luigi replied:

'Could be.'

'Have you seen him recently?'

Maigret had asked the question with his most innocent air, glass in hand, looking off in another direction. He knew Luigi and Luigi knew him. The two men liked each other. But the atmosphere had changed in a split second.

'Is he in Paris?'

'I think so.'

'How come you're interested in him?'

'Oh, just by the by . . .'

'I've never seen Charlie Cinaglia in the flesh, because I'd left the States before he made a name for himself. I haven't heard anything about him coming to Europe.'

'I was thinking someone might have mentioned him to you. He's been to Pozzo's a few times. And you're both Italian by birth.'

'I am Neapolitan,' Luigi corrected him.

'And Pozzo?'

'Sicilian. It's a bit like confusing someone from Marseille with a Corsican.'

'I wonder who Charlie has been in touch with besides Pozzo since he got to Paris. He didn't come on his own. Tony Cicero's with him.'

This was when Luigi filled his glass for the second time. Maigret seemed a little vague, talked listlessly, without conviction. As Lucas, who knew him well, put it, he was going fishing. Sometimes he managed to seem so innocuous that even his right-hand men were taken in.

'It all seems damn complicated,' he sighed. 'Not to mention that there's another American mixed up in the whole thing, Bill Larner.'

'Bill hasn't got anything to do with the others,' Luigi said quickly. 'Bill is a gentleman.'

'One of your customers?'

'He comes from time to time.'

'Supposing Bill Larner needed to hide, where do you think he'd go?'

'Supposing, as you say, because I don't think it would ever happen, Bill would hide out somewhere he couldn't be found. But take it from me, Bill has nothing to do with those other two.'

'Do you know Cicero?'

'His name sometimes appears in the American papers.'

'A gangster?'

'Are you really interested in these people?'

Luigi was already cooler. He might have been Neapolitan rather than Sicilian, but his tone and the way he was looking at Maigret were starting to recall Pozzo.

'You've been to the United States, haven't you? Then you should understand that these aren't matters for the French police. The Americans themselves, apart from a few in the FBI, are out of their depth with these organizations. I don't know why the people you're talking about have come to Paris, if they have. I mean, you say they have, so I'm quite happy to believe you, but I'm surprised all the same. In any case what they're up to is no concern of yours.'

'What if they'd killed a man?'

'A Frenchman?'

'I don't know.'

'If they've killed someone, then they were contracted to do so, and you'll never be able to prove anything against them. Not that I know either of them. The first two you told me about are Sicilians. As for Bill Larner, I still say that he has nothing in common with them.'

'When Cicero's in the American papers, what's it in connection with?'

'Extortion rackets, generally. You wouldn't understand. There aren't any genuine criminal organizations here like the ones they've got over there. You don't even have real killers here. Suppose a guy in Paris goes round the shopkeepers in his neighbourhood telling them they need protection against hoodlums and that he's going to take care of it from now on for so many thousand francs a week. The shopkeepers would just go to the police, wouldn't they? Or they'd burst out laughing. Well, no one laughs in America, and only fools go to the police. Because if they do, or if they don't pay up, a bomb goes off in their shop, if they're not machine-gunned on their way home, that is.'

Luigi was growing animated. Like Pozzo, you would have sworn that he was proud of his fellow countrymen.

'That's not all. Suppose one of these guys is arrested. There'll almost always be a judge or high-ranking politician to get him released. But let's say for the sake of argument that the sheriff or district attorney digs his heels in. Ten witnesses will immediately come forward to swear on oath that the poor lad was at the other end of town at the time. And if an honest witness claims the opposite, if he is crazy enough to stand by his statement, he'll have an accident before the day of the trial. Got it?'

A tall man with blond hair had just come in and was leaning on the bar a few metres away from Maigret and Lucas. Luigi winked at him.

'Martini?'

'Martini,' repeated the customer, looking at the two Frenchmen with an amused expression.

Maigret had already blown his nose a couple of times. His nose tickled. His eyelids felt hot. Had he caught Lognon's cold?

Lucas, meanwhile, decent soul that he was, was waiting for a reaction from his boss. But Maigret let Luigi hold forth as if he had nothing to say.

The truth is he was starting to lose patience. For Pozzo to advise him to drop it was one thing. But for Luigi to say pretty much the same thing here, in this elegant bar, was getting a bit much.

'Suppose, inspector, an American shows up in Marseille and tries to go after the underworld there. Eh? What would happen to him? Well, they're kids in Marseille compared to . . .'

All right! All right! Who knows? If Maigret had looked up the American consul or ambassador, maybe those gentlemen would also have chorused, 'Don't get involved, Maigret. It's not for you.'

Not for the kindergarten, eh! He almost felt like saying, which would obviously have been pretty ridiculous, 'What about Landru, was that kindergarten games too?'

He had drained his drink in sullen silence, well aware that a disappointed Lucas was wondering why he wasn't putting Luigi in his place.

Now that they were out on the street, Lucas still hadn't dared ask him anything. Maigret made no mention of taking a taxi or a bus. He just walked grimly along with his hands in his pockets. They had already gone a long way when, turning to his colleague, Maigret said in all seriousness, as if he had doubted himself up until that moment:

'What do you bet I'll get them?'

'I'm sure of it,' Lucas replied hastily.

'And I'm positive! You understand? Positive! Those . . .'

It was rare for Maigret to use a truly offensive word, but he uttered that one with relief.

Nothing might come of it, but he had sent Lucas over to Rue des Acacias to keep an eye on Pozzo's restaurant all the same.

'There's no point hiding, our friend is smart enough to spot you. He won't have telephoned, because he knows the line is tapped, but if he's had the chance he's bound to have told the two guys who were in his bar yesterday evening and who warned Charlie and Cicero. There's still a slight possibility, though, that he hasn't been able to get in touch with them. In that case, one of the two will come to Rue des Acacias.'

He had described them to Lucas, given him detailed instructions. Back at Quai des Orfèvres, he went straight up to the laboratory without looking in at his office.

Moers was waiting for him, eating a sandwich. He immediately turned on a slide projector that looked like a huge magic lantern, and an image showed up on the screen.

It was the marks Pozzo's pencil had left on the notepad. The first letters were relatively clear: G A L. After that came some numbers.

'As you thought, chief, it's a telephone number. The exchange is Galvani. The first number is a 2, the second a 7, the third's impossible to make out, so is the fourth: it might be a 0, but I'm not sure, or a 9, or a 6.'

Moers was giving Maigret odd looks as well, not because he smelled of alcohol but because he seemed vague. And as he left he came out with a word he hardly ever used except at moments like this, 'Thanks, *son!*'

He went to his office, took off his overcoat, opened the door to the inspectors' office.

'Janvier, Lapointe . . .'

Before giving them instructions, he telephoned the Brasserie Dauphine.

'Have you eaten, you two?'

'Yes, chief.'

He ordered sandwiches for himself and beer for the three of them.

'Each of you take a list of telephone numbers. Look under Galvani.'

It was a massive job. Unless they were incredibly lucky, it would take the two men hours to find the right number.

The customers who were playing poker dice at Pozzo's had left just after they had started eating – in other words, three-quarters of an hour, or even an hour, before Maigret and Lognon had themselves left. Pozzo had told them to telephone a Galvani number. That covered the area around Avenue de la Grande-Armée. And wasn't Avenue de la Grande-Armée exactly where the car had been stolen that had taken Lognon to Saint-Germain forest?

It all connected. Either the three Americans were together when they had been warned, or else they had been able to meet up quickly, because an hour later they were on the lookout near the restaurant.

'Are we after a hotel, chief?'

'I've no idea. Maybe. At any rate they won't have stayed in a hotel under their real names. If they're in one, they've managed to get fake identity cards or passports.'

It wasn't out of the question. Someone like Pozzo was bound to know the ropes.

'I don't think they're in a hotel or a boarding house, though, because they'll know we put those under surveillance first.'

How about with a friend of Larner's, because Larner had been in Paris for two years and must have contacts? In that case they were most likely to be with a woman.

'Try all the numbers that seem to fit. Compile a list of single women with Italian or American names.'

He wasn't under any illusions. Even if they happened on the right number, the birds would already have flown. Pozzo wasn't an innocent or a novice. He had seen Maigret take the notepad. He would have sounded the alarm again by now.

Maigret telephoned his wife, who was expecting him for dinner, then Madame Lognon, who bemoaned her situation in more detail.

The door between his and the inspectors' office was open. He could hear Janvier and Lapointe telephoning different numbers, telling a different story each time, as he gradually curled up in his chair, puffing ever more sparingly on his pipe.

He wasn't asleep, though. He was hot. He felt he had a slight fever. With his eyes half-closed, he was trying to think, but his train of thought was becoming more and more hazy, and he kept coming back to the same rallying cry: 'I'm going to get them!'

How he would get them was another story. To tell the truth, he didn't have the slightest idea, but he had rarely been as determined to see a job through in his life. It was almost a matter of national interest, as far as he was concerned, and everything about it, even the word gangster, drove him mad.

'... Oh absolutely, Monsieur Luigi! Absolutely, Monsieur Pozzo! Absolutely, my American friends! None of you are going to make me change my mind. I've always said that killers are idiots, and I will keep saying it. If they weren't, they wouldn't kill anyone. Understood? No? You're not convinced? Well, I, Maigret, will prove it to you. There! That's all! Now, get out!'

When the office boy knocked at the door and, getting no answer, opened it a crack, Maigret was sleeping with his pipe dangling from his lips.

'An express letter, inspector.'

It was the photographs and information sent by plane from Washington.

Ten minutes later the laboratory was printing off copies of the photographs. At four o'clock the journalists were assembled in the waiting room, and Maigret was giving each of them a set of proofs.

'Don't ask me what they're wanted for, just help me find them. Run the photographs on the front page. Anyone who has seen one of these men is requested to telephone my office immediately.'

'Are they armed?'

Maigret hesitated, then decided to reply honestly:

'They're not only armed, they're dangerous.'

Using the term that was starting to get on his nerves, he went on, 'They're killers. Or one of them is, at least.'

The photographs were being wired to all railway stations, border points and police brigades.

All this, as poor Lognon would have said, was the easy part. Lucas was still cooling his heels in Rue des Acacias. Janvier and Lapointe were calling telephone numbers. Whenever they found a vaguely suspicious number, someone would go and check it.

At five o'clock he was told that Washington wanted him on the telephone, and he heard MacDonald greet him with a genial 'Jules'.

'Look here, Jules, I've been thinking about your call and I've managed to have a quick chat about it with the big boss . . .'

Maigret might have been imagining it, but he thought MacDonald sounded more guarded than the day before. There were long pauses.

'Yes, I'm listening.'

'Are you sure that Cinaglia and Cicero are in Paris?'

'Positive. I've just had it confirmed from photographs by someone who has seen them close up.'

It was true. He had sent a detective to Madame Lognon's, and she had been adamant.

'Hello?'

'Yes, I'm still here.'

'Are there only two of them?'

'They've got in touch with Bill Larner.'

'He's not important, as I said before. Have they met up with anyone else?'

'That's what I'm trying to establish.'

MacDonald seemed to be beating around the bush, as if he were afraid of saying too much.

'You haven't heard anything about a third Sicilian?'

'Called?'

Another hesitation.

'Mascarelli.'

'Would he have got here at the same time as the others?'

'Definitely not. A few weeks earlier.'

'I'll have someone look up the name in our hotel records.'

'Mascarelli probably isn't registered under his own name.'

'In that case . . .'

'Have a look anyway. If you hear of a Mascarelli, known as Sloppy Joe, let me know by telephone. I'll give you his description. Short and thin, looks fifty although he's only forty-one, unhealthy looking, with boil scars on his neck. Do you know what the word sloppy means?'

Maigret did but he would have had difficulty finding an exact equivalent in French: someone not very crisp or clean, badly dressed.

'Good. That's his nickname, and he lives up to it.'

'What's he doing in France?'

A silence on the other end of the line.

'What are the other two doing here?'

MacDonald said something in a low voice, as if he was asking advice from someone standing near him, then answered finally, 'If Charlie Cinaglia and Cicero met Sloppy Joe in Paris, there's every likelihood the body your inspector saw being thrown out of a car was Sloppy Joe.'

'That's crystal clear, obviously,' Maigret said mockingly.

'I'm sorry, Jules, but it's more or less all I know myself.'

Maigret called Le Havre, then Cherbourg, and got through to the official in charge of arrivals at each port. They checked their passenger lists without finding anyone by the name of Mascarelli. Maigret gave them as full a description as he could and they promised to question their inspectors.

Janvier appeared.

'Torrence is asking for you on the telephone, chief.'

'Where is he?'

'Around Grande-Armée, checking addresses.'

It didn't make any sense for him to come back to Quai des Orfèvres between visits. He would ring with the results from a bar, then be given another address.

'Hello? Is that you, chief? I'm calling from the apartment of a woman who I'd rather not let out of my sight. I think you'd better come over and have a word with her. She's hard work.'

Maigret vaguely heard a woman's voice, then Torrence's, no longer talking into the telephone, 'If you don't keep quiet, you'll get a slap in the face. Are you there, chief? I'm at 28A, Rue Brunel. It's the fourth floor, on the left. The woman's name is Adrienne Laur. It might be a good idea to see if the name's in Records.'

Maigret put Lapointe on it, then, donning his heavy overcoat and gathering up a couple of pipes from his desk, headed for the stairs. He was lucky enough to find one of the police cars in the courtyard.

'Rue Brunel.'

Still the same neighbourhood, not far from Avenue Wagram, barely 200 metres from Rue des Acacias and 300 from where the car had been stolen the previous evening. The apartment building was comfortable, bourgeois. There was a lift, carpets on the stairs. When he got to the fourth floor, a door opened, and the hefty figure of Torrence appeared, looking relieved.

'Maybe you'll get something out of her, chief. I give up.'

A woman with brown hair and a fullish figure was standing in the middle of the living room, wearing nothing but a dressing gown that opened every time she moved.

'Two now!' she said sarcastically. 'How many of you are after me?'

Maigret had politely taken off his hat and put it on an armchair. As it was very hot, he also took off his overcoat, murmuring:

'Do you mind?'

'I mind the whole thing, as you may have noticed.'

She was a beautiful woman, really, in her thirties, with the slightly hoarse voice of people whose nights are busier than their days. The room smelled of perfume. The bedroom door was open, revealing an unmade bed. There was a pillow on a sofa in the living room, and another on the floor in a corner, where a couple of rugs had been piled on top of one another.

Torrence, who had followed Maigret's gaze, said:

'Get it, chief?'

She obviously hadn't been the only person sleeping in the apartment the previous night.

'When I rang the bell, she took a long time answering. She says she was asleep. She could have been. She must have been sleeping completely naked because she hasn't got a stitch on under her dressing gown.'

'Is that any of your business?'

'I asked her if she knew an American called Bill Larner and I saw she was hesitating, playing for time, pretending to rack her brains. She put up a fight, but I went in and glanced in the bedroom. Have a look for yourself. On the chest of drawers to the left.'

There was a photograph in a red leather frame, probably taken at Deauville, of a couple in swimming costumes: Adrienne Laur and Bill Larner.

'You see why I rang you? That's not all. Have a look in the wastepaper basket. I counted eight cigar butts. They are those big Havanas that each last a good hour. I suppose when I rang she saw the full ashtrays and quickly emptied them in the wastepaper bin.'

'I had some friends over yesterday evening.'

'How many friends?'

'That's none of your business.'

'Bill Larner?'

'That's none of your business either. Besides, that photo was taken a year ago, and we've split up since.'

There was a bottle of brandy and a glass on a chest of drawers. She poured herself a drink without offering them one, then lit a fresh cigarette and fluffed up her hair at the back.

'Am I going to be allowed to go back to bed?'

'Listen, my girl . . .'

'I'm not your girl.'

'You'd be better off answering me nicely.'

'Oh, really!'

'You thought you were doing the right thing. Larner asked you to put him up, along with his two friends. He probably didn't tell you why.'

'You've got a lovely voice, sweetie.'

Torrence's look seemed to say: 'You see what she's like?'

Maigret patiently asked, 'Are you French, Adrienne?'

'She's Belgian,' Torrence put in. 'I found her identity card in her bag. She was born in Antwerp and has lived in France for five years.'

'In other words we can take away your resident's card. I suppose you work in cabarets?'

'She's one of the Folies-Bergère nudes.'

Torrence was still doing all the talking.

'So? Just because I'm a nude dancer you have the right to barge into my place as if it's a stable, do you? You, fatso,' she pointed at Torrence, 'if I hadn't snatched your hat off your head, you wouldn't even have bothered to take it off. But every time my dressing gown opens, I know where you're looking.'

'Listen, Adrienne, I don't know what Larner has said, but he probably hasn't told you the truth about his friends. Do you speak English?'

'Enough for what I need it for.'

'The two men who slept here are wanted for murder. Do you understand? That means that, because you put them up, you could be prosecuted for aiding and abetting. Do you know how much you'll get for that?'

He had hit a raw nerve. She had stopped pacing about, was looking at him anxiously.

'Five to ten years.'

'I haven't done anything.'

'I'm sure you haven't, and that's why I said you're making a mistake. It's fine helping friends as long as you don't have to pay too high a price.'

'You're trying to get me to talk.'

'The shorter of the two men with Bill is called Charlie.'

She didn't deny it.

'The other is Tony Cicero.'

'I don't know them. I know Bill's never killed anyone.'

'I know that too. In fact I'm convinced that Bill wasn't helping them of his own free will.'

'Are you serious?'

She looked at the bottle, poured herself another half a glass, almost offered one to Maigret, then shrugged.

'I've known Larner for years,' he said.

'He's only been in France for a couple.'

'But his details have been on our files for fifteen. As someone put it this morning, he's a gentleman.'

She was staring at him, frowning, in two minds as to whether he was setting a trap for her.

'Charlie and Cicero have been hiding in your apartment for at least two days, probably three. Do you have a refrigerator?'

Torrence cut in again.

'I thought of that. I found one in the kitchen. It's full. Two cold chickens, half a ham, practically a whole salami . . .'

'Yesterday evening,' Maigret went on, 'someone gave them a message by telephone, and all three of them left in a hurry.'

She sat down in an armchair and, with unexpected modesty, arranged her dressing gown over her legs and thighs.

'They came back in the night. I am sure they'd been drinking. From what I know of Bill Larner, he must have been drinking heavily because he had just witnessed a scene that would have put him on edge.'

Torrence was pacing up and down the apartment, so she shouted:

'Can't you just stay still?'

Then she turned to Maigret:

'What else?'

'I don't know what time this morning they got another message. Not before eleven o'clock, at any rate. They were probably asleep, Bill in your bed, the other two in this room. They hurriedly got dressed. Did they tell you where they were going?'

'You're trying to get me into trouble.'

'The opposite. I'm trying to get you out of it!'

'Are you the Maigret who's in the papers the whole time?'

'Why?'

'Because they say you're on the level. But I don't like this tub of lard.'

'What did they say to you when they left?'

'Nothing. Not even thank you.'

'How did Bill seem?'

'I haven't admitted Bill was here.'

'You must have heard what they were saying when they were getting ready to leave.'

'They were talking English.'

'I thought you knew English?'

'Not that kind.'

'Last night, when he was alone with you in your bedroom, Bill talked to you about his friends.'

'How do you know that?'

'Didn't he tell you he was trying to get rid of them?'

'He said that he'd take them to the country as soon as he could.'

'Where?'

'I don't know.'

'Did he often go to the country?'

'Hardly ever.'

'Did you ever go there together?'

'No.'

'Were you his mistress?'

'On and off.'

'Have you been to his apartment in the Hôtel Wagram?'

'Once. I found him there with a girl. He threw me out. Then three days later he came to see me as if nothing had happened.'

'Does he fish?'

She laughed.

'You mean with a rod? No! That's not his style.'

'Does he play golf?'

'Yes, he does that.'

'Where?'

'I don't know. I've never gone with him.'

'Did he used to go for a few days?'

'He'd leave in the morning and come back in the evening.'

That didn't fit. He had to find a place where Larner had a habit of staying overnight.

'Apart from the two men who slept here, did he ever introduce you to any of his friends?'

'Not really.'

'What sort of friends did he have?'

'Mainly people from the racing world, jockeys, trainers.'

Torrence and Maigret exchanged a glance. They sensed they were getting warmer.

'Did he bet on the races a lot?'

'Yes.'

'For high stakes?'

'Yes.'

'Did he win?'

'Almost always. He got tips.'

'From jockeys and trainers?'

'That's what I understood.'

'Did he ever talk to you about Maisons-Laffitte?'

'He telephoned me once from there.'

'At night?'

'At the end of the show.'

'To ask you to go and meet him?'

'The opposite. To tell me he couldn't see me.'

'Did he have to spend the night there?'

'I suppose.'

'At an inn?'

'He didn't say.'

'Thank you, Adrienne. I'm sorry to have disturbed you.'

She seemed surprised that he wasn't taking her with him and found it hard to believe that they hadn't been laying a trap for her.

'Which of them did the killing?' she asked when Maigret's hand was already on the doorknob.

'Charlie. Does that surprise you?'

'No. But I like the other one even less. He's as cold as a crocodile.'

She didn't respond to Torrence's wave but smiled vaguely at Maigret, who gave an almost formal bow.

On the way downstairs, Maigret said to his colleague:

'We'll have to get her telephone tapped. Not that anything will come of it. These guys are on their guard.'

Then, remembering Pozzo's and Luigi's insistent warnings about the killers, he added:

'You'd better keep an eye on her. She's not a bad girl, and it would be a pity if anything happened to her.'

Pozzo's restaurant was just around the corner, with Lucas still on duty nearby. Maigret had the car drive down Rue des Acacias.

'Nothing to report?'

'One of the guys you described to me, one of the ones playing poker dice, went in a quarter of an hour ago.'

They were directly opposite the restaurant. Maigret allowed himself the pleasure of calmly getting out of the car, pushing open the door and touching the brim of his hat.

'Hello, Pozzo.'

Then, turning to the customer sitting at the bar, he said:

'Identity card, please.'

The guy looked like a nightclub musician or gigolo. He hesitated, seemingly looking to Pozzo for guidance, but Pozzo was looking the other way.

Maigret wrote down his name and address in his notebook.

Strangely he wasn't Italian or American but Spanish, and, according to his papers, an opera singer by profession. He lived in a little hotel on Avenue des Ternes.

'Thank you.'

Maigret gave back the card, didn't ask any questions and touched the brim of his hat once more. The Spaniard and Pozzo watched him leave in amazement.

5.

In which, while a certain Baron goes out on the prowl, Maigret makes the mistake of going to the cinema

Snugly wrapped up in his overcoat in the back of the car, Maigret was watching the lights go past, thinking. As they crossed Place de la Concorde, he told the driver, 'Make a detour via Rue des Capucines. I've got a telephone call to make.'

He needed to call Quai des Orfèvres. It would only have taken five minutes to go straight there, but he quite liked the thought of revisiting the Manhattan in a different frame of mind to this morning, and, besides, having recovered his taste for whiskey without too much hardship, he wasn't averse to having another.

The place was full, with at least thirty faces lined up along the bar in a pall of cigarette smoke. Everyone, or almost everyone, was talking English, and a few customers were engrossed in American newspapers. Luigi and his two assistants were busy mixing drinks.

'The same whiskey as this morning,' Maigret said, and the bar owner was struck by his calm, cheerful demeanour.

'Bourbon?'

'You were the one who served me. I don't know.'

Luigi didn't seem pleased to see him, and Maigret thought he saw him quickly scan the room, as if he wanted to check nobody was there whom Maigret shouldn't see.

'Tell me, Luigi . . .'

'Just a moment . . .'

He was pouring drinks left and right, busying himself unnecessarily as if he was trying to put off the policeman's questions.

'I was saying, Luigi, that there's another of your countrymen I'd like to meet. Have you heard of someone called Mascarelli, also known as Sloppy Joe?'

He had spoken in a normal voice while those around him were shouting to make themselves heard. But now at least ten people were looking at him curiously. He felt slightly like the man at a gathering of old ladies who has gone too far with a smutty joke.

Luigi said flatly:

'Don't know him, don't want to either.'

Satisfied, Maigret headed to the phone booth.

'Is that you, Janvier? Will you see if the Baron is still in the building? If he is, ask him to wait for me. If he isn't, try to get hold of him on the telephone and ask him to come to headquarters as soon as possible. I need to see him urgently.'

He threaded his way between the groups of people standing around, drinking. As he went to finish his whiskey, he caught sight of a face he had seen before. It was a tall, blond-haired fellow who looked as if he was straight out of an American film and who was following the inspector with his eyes.

Luigi was too busy to say goodbye, and Maigret went back to his car. A quarter of an hour later, when he walked into his office, a man sitting in the only armchair leaped to his feet.

It was the Baron, so called not because he had a title but because that was his surname. He didn't belong to Maigret's squad. For twenty-five years he had specialized in the racetracks, preferring to remain an inspector all his life rather than change jobs.

'You sent for me, detective chief inspector?'

'Sit down, my friend. One moment . . .'

Maigret took off his overcoat, went next door to see if there were any messages for him and finally took a seat and filled his pipe.

After years of going to the races, where he concentrated exclusively on the regulars in the enclosure, rather than the small fry in the public stands, the Baron had started to resemble the race-goers. Like them, he wore a pair of binoculars slung over his shoulder and, on Arc de Triomphe day, sported a pearl-grey bowler and matching spats. Some people claimed to have seen him in a monocle, which may have been true. It may also have been true, as was rumoured, that he had developed a passion for betting himself.

'I'm going to explain the situation and you can tell me what you think.'

In his career Maigret had worked in almost all the departments – Traffic, Railways, Department Stores, and even, to his extreme displeasure, the Vice Squad – but he had never had anything to do with the races.

'Suppose an American who's been living in Paris for a couple of years and is a regular at the track . . .'

'What sort of American?'

'Not the sort invited to parties at the embassy. A major-league crook, Bill Larner.'

'I know him,' the Baron said calmly.

'Good. That makes things easier. For certain reasons, Larner had to go into hiding this morning with two of his countrymen, who have just got off the boat and don't speak a word of French. They know that we have their descriptions, and I doubt they've taken a train or plane. I actually doubt they've gone very far from Paris. Something seems to be keeping them here. They haven't got a car, but they've got a knack of stealing the first one they come across and dumping it afterwards.'

The Baron was listening attentively, like a specialist who had been called in for a consultation.

'I've often run into Larner with a pretty woman on his arm,' he said.

'I know. He and his two friends were actually hiding out with one of them until today. I doubt he'll make the same play twice, though.'

'I agree. He's smart.'

'I've heard, from that girl in fact, that he has friends in the racing world. You see what I'm getting at? He had to make a decision fast, come up with a safe hiding place in minutes. It is more than likely that he asked one of his fellow countrymen. Do you know many Americans in the racing world?'

'There are some. Not as many as English, of course. Hang on, I'm thinking of a jockey, little Lope, but no, he'll be racing in Miami at the moment. I've also met a trainer, Teddy Brown, who runs one of his countrymen's stables. There are definitely others.'

'Hold on, Baron, the guy I am thinking of has to live somewhere secure. I think you need to put yourself in Bill Larner's shoes and ask yourself where would be a secure place to hide. Apparently he's spent the odd night at Maisons-Laffitte, or near there.'

'That's not such a bad idea.'

'What isn't?'

'There's quite a few stables round there. Do you need an immediate answer?'

'As soon as possible.'

'In that case I'd need to nose around some bars I know to refresh my memory. These sorts come and go. If I have an answer tonight, where will you be?'

'At home.'

He strode self-importantly to the door. After a brief hesitation, Maigret stopped him.

'One other thing. Be careful. When you get a lead, don't follow it up yourself. We're dealing with killers.'

He couldn't help saying this word in a slightly ironic way, having had it endlessly drummed into him in the last forty-eight hours.

'Understood. I'll almost certainly ring you this evening. In any case, I'll have something tomorrow morning. It doesn't matter if it cost a few rounds of drinks, does it?'

When Maigret got to Boulevard Richard-Lenoir, he found Madame Maigret dressed to go out. He had been meaning to go to bed with a hot toddy and some aspirin to bring down the cold, which was starting to get on his nerves, but he remembered it was Friday, which was their day for the cinema.

'Lognon?' asked his wife.

He had the latest. The final verdict was that Inspector Hard-Done-By was suffering from full-blown pneumonia, which the doctors hoped to arrest with penicillin. They were more worried about the blow he had received to his head.

'There's no fracture, but they are afraid of trauma to the brain. By about four o'clock, he didn't really know what he was saying.'

'How is his wife?'

'She claims that they have no right to separate a couple who have been married thirty years and insists that either he be taken home or that she be allowed to stay in the hospital.'

'Are they letting her?'

'No.'

They were in the habit of strolling peacefully arm in arm to Boulevard Bonne-Nouvelle, and it didn't take them long to choose a cinema. Maigret wasn't fussy about films; in fact he always preferred a routine offering to some big studio production. Settling down in his seat, he would watch the images go by without worrying too much about the story. When he was in a down-to-earth cinema, in a thick fug of smoke, surrounded by people laughing at the good bits and eating chocolate ice creams and peanuts, and lovers kissing, he couldn't be happier.

It was still cold and damp. When they came out of the cinema, they sat on a café terrace by a brazier and had a glass of beer, and it was eleven o'clock when they opened the door of the apartment and heard the telephone ringing.

'Hello! Baron?'

'It's Vacher here, inspector. I came on duty at eight. I've been trying to reach you since nine.'

'Is there any news?'

'There's an express letter for you. A woman's handwriting. It has *very urgent* written in big letters. Do you want me to open it and read it to you?'

'Please.'

'Just a moment. Here we are:

Detective chief inspector,

I have to see you as soon as possible. It is a matter of life or death. I'm afraid I can't leave my room and I don't even know how I'll get this message to you. Can you come and see me at the Hôtel de Bretagne, Rue Richer, almost directly opposite the Folies-Bergère? I am in Room 47. Don't tell anyone. There's probably someone watching the hotel.

Come, I beg you.'

The barely legible signature started with an M.

'Probably Mado,' said Vacher. 'I'm not sure.'

'What time was the letter sent?'

'At ten past eight.'

'I'm on my way. Anything else? Any news from Lucas and Torrence?'

'Lucas is at Pozzo's restaurant. Apparently Pozzo called him in, saying it was stupid standing on the pavement when it was warmer inside. He's asking for instructions.'

'Tell him to go to bed.'

Madame Maigret, who had been listening, merely sighed as Maigret looked for his hat. She was used to it.

'Do you think you'll come home tonight? In any case, you'd better take a scarf.'

He had a nip of sloe gin before leaving, then had to walk all the way to République before finding a taxi.

'Rue Richer, opposite the Folies-Bergère.'

He knew the Hôtel de Bretagne, the first two floors of which were reserved for what the owners called *casuals*, prostitutes who brought in customers for an hour or less. The other rooms were rented by the week or month.

The theatre had closed its doors, and the street was deserted except for a few persistent women pacing up and down.

'Want to go somewhere?'

He shrugged, entered a dimly lit hallway and knocked on a glass door to the right. A light came on.

'Who is it?' a voice muttered sleepily.

'Room 47.'

'Go on up . . .'

Behind the curtain, he could vaguely make out a man lying on a camp bed near the key rack. The man reached for a rubber bulb switch that opened the second door, then his hand froze in mid-air. He had needed a minute to come to; the number 47 hadn't meant anything to him at first.

'Nobody's there,' he grunted, lying back down.

'Wait a moment. I need to talk to you.'

'What do you want?'

'Police!'

Maigret thought better of trying to understand the mutterings this provoked, which were clearly less than friendly. In his cubbyhole, the man got up from the bed where he had been sleeping fully dressed. Grim-faced, he came towards the glass door and turned the key in the lock. When he finally set eyes on Maigret, he frowned.

'You're not from Vice, are you?'

'How do you know there's no one in 47?'

'Because the guy left several days ago, and I saw the woman go out a moment ago.'

'When?'

'I don't know exactly. Maybe around nine thirty.'

'Is she called Mado?'

The night porter shrugged.

'I only work nights and I don't know people's names. She gave in her key as she went out. Look, there it is on the board.'

'Was the lady on her own?'

He didn't answer immediately.

'I'm asking you if the lady was on her own.'

'What do you want from her? All right, no need to lose your temper! Somebody went up to see her a little earlier.'

'A man?'

The porter was stunned that, in an establishment like that, someone could be naive enough to ask him such a question.

'How long was he up there?'

'About ten minutes.'

'Did he ask for her room number?'

'He didn't ask anything at all. He went straight up without even looking at me. At that time, the doors aren't locked.'

'How do you know he went up to 47?'

'Because he came back down with her.'

'Have you got their check-in forms?'

'No. The landlady keeps them in her office, which is locked.'

'Where is she?'

'In bed, with the landlord.'

'Give me the key and go and wake her up. Tell her to come and meet me upstairs.'

The man gave Maigret an odd look, then sighed:

'You don't give up, do you? Can you prove you're a policeman, at least?'

Maigret showed him his badge, then set off up the stairs, room key in hand. Room 47 was on the fifth floor; it was unremarkable: an iron bed, a washstand, a bidet, a rickety armchair and a chest of drawers.

The bed hadn't been slept in. On the dubious-looking bedspread, a newspaper was opened out with the photographs of Charlie Cinaglia and Cicero on the front page. It was the evening edition, published around six o'clock. Anyone coming across the two men was requested as a matter of urgency to inform Detective Chief Inspector Maigret.

Was this why the woman who appeared to be called Mado had sent him an express letter?

In a corner of the room there were two suitcases: one old and battered, the other brand new. Both bore the labels of a Canadian shipping company. They weren't locked. Maigret opened them and began spreading out their contents on the bed: women's underwear and clothing, mainly new, bought in Montreal.

'Don't mind me,' said a voice at the door.

It was the landlady of the hotel, breathless from climbing the stairs. She was small and tough, and her grey hair in metal curlers did nothing for her looks.

'For a start, who are you?'

'Detective Chief Inspector Maigret, Crime Squad.'

'What do you want?'

'To find out about the woman staying in this room.'

'Why? What has she done?'

'I'd give me her form and not argue, if I was you.'

She had brought it just in case but still only handed it over reluctantly.

'You lot, you'll never learn manners.'

She headed towards a connecting door, which was half open, clearly intending to shut it.

'Wait a moment. Who's staying in the next room?'

'The lady's husband. Is that forbidden?'

'Leave the door alone. I see the couple are signed in under the name of Perkins: Monsieur et Madame Perkins of Montreal, Canada.'

'So?'

'Have you looked at their passports?'

'I wouldn't have let them stay if they hadn't been in order.'

'According to this form they arrived a month ago.'

'Is that a problem?'

'Can you describe John Perkins to me?'

'A short, brown-haired man, in poor health, with eye trouble.'

'Why do you say he has eye trouble?'

'Because he always wore sunglasses, even at night. Has he done something wrong?'

'How was he dressed?'

'Brand new clothes from head to toe. It's pretty common for newlyweds, isn't it?'

'Are they newlyweds?'

'I guess so.'

'What makes you think that?'

'They almost never left their rooms.'

'Why did they have two rooms?'

'That's none of my business.'

'Where did they have their meals?'

'I didn't ask. Monsieur Perkins must have eaten here because I don't think I ever saw him go out during the day, especially not recently.'

'What do you mean by recently?'

'In the last week. Or the last couple of weeks.'

'Didn't he ever go out for some fresh air?'

'Only in the evening.'

'Wearing sunglasses?'

'I'm telling you what I saw. Too bad if you don't believe me.'

'Did his wife go out?'

'She'd go out to buy him something to eat. Once I even went up to check they weren't cooking, because we don't allow that here.'

'So he made do with cold food for weeks.'

'Looks like it.'

'Didn't you think that was strange?'

'Foreigners do stranger things than that.'

'The night porter told me that Perkins left the hotel a few days ago. Can you remember when you saw him last?'

'I don't know. Sunday or Monday.'

'Did he take any luggage?'

'No.'

'Did he say he was going to be gone for a while?'

'He didn't say anything at all. He could have told me whatever he wanted, and I wouldn't have understood, because he didn't speak a word of French.'

'What about his wife?'

'She speaks it like you and me.'

'Without an accent?'

'With something like a Belgian accent. Apparently that's what a Canadian accent sounds like.'

'Did they have Canadian passports?'

'Yes.'

'How did you know that Perkins had left?'

'He went for a walk one evening, Sunday or Monday, as I've told you, and the following morning Lucile, who does the rooms on this floor, told me he'd gone, and that his wife seemed worried. If you're going to be asking me questions for much longer, I should have a seat.'

She sat down in a dignified way and looked at him reproachfully.

'Did the Perkins have visitors?'

'Not that I know.'

'Where's the telephone?'

'In the office, where I am all day. They never made telephone calls, either of them.'

'Did they have post?'

'They didn't get a single letter.'

'Did Madame Perkins pick up any from the post office?'

'I didn't follow her. Hey, are you sure you're allowed to search through their belongings?'

While he was talking, Maigret had carried on emptying the two suitcases, the contents of which were now spread out on the bed.

Neither cheap nor expensive, the clothes were relatively good quality. The shoes had exaggeratedly high heels, and the underwear would have been more suited to a nightclub hostess than a newlywed.

'I'd like to see next door.'

'You might as well!'

She went in after him, as though to stop him taking anything. Here too there were new suitcases, bought in Montreal, and all the men's clothes were new and had Canadian labels. It was as though the couple had suddenly decided to reinvent themselves and had snapped up everything they needed for their trip in a matter of hours. On the chest of drawers lay a dozen or so of the sort of

American newspapers you can generally only find at a few stands on Place de l'Opéra and Place de la Madeleine.

No photographs. No papers. At the very bottom of one of the suitcases Maigret found a passport in the name of Mr and Mrs John Perkins of Montreal, Canada. According to the visas and stamps, the couple had embarked six weeks earlier in Halifax, disembarked in Southampton and then entered France via Dieppe.

'Have you got what you wanted?'

'Does Lucile, the maid, live in the hotel?'

'Her room's on the seventh floor.'

'Ask her to come down.'

'Why not? It's so handy being in the police, isn't it. You can wake people up at any hour of the night, disturb their sleep . . .'

She carried on talking to herself as she went up the stairs.

Maigret discovered a bottle of blue ink that had been used to write the express letter. He also found some cold meat left on the window ledge to keep it cool.

Lucile was a small, dark woman with a squint, who had a habit of letting one of her limp breasts repeatedly slip out of her sky-blue dressing gown.

'I don't need you any more,' Maigret told the landlady. 'You can go back to bed.'

'You're too kind. Don't let him intimidate you, Lucile.'

Lucile wasn't remotely intimidated. The door had barely closed before she said almost ecstatically:

'Is it true that you're the famous Inspector Maigret?'

'Sit down, Lucile. I'd like you to tell me everything you know about the Perkins.'

'I always thought they were a strange couple.'

She found it in herself to blush.

'Don't you find it strange, people having separate bedrooms when they're married?'

'Didn't they ever sleep in the same bed?'

'Never.'

'Are you sure they didn't get together at night?'

'Us maids, you see, can tell by the state of the bed in the morning if . . .'

She blushed even more deeply, temporarily tucking her breast back into her dressing gown.

'In other words, you had the impression that they didn't sleep together?'

'I am pretty sure they didn't.'

'What time do you do the rooms?'

'That depends what day it is. Sometimes around nine in the morning, sometimes in the afternoon. With her room, I waited as far as possible until she went out. But he was always in his.'

'How did he pass the time?'

'Reading his big newspapers with their hundreds of pages, doing crosswords or writing letters.'

'Did you see him write letters?'

'Yes. Quite often.'

'Didn't he ever go out during the day?'

'Only at the start. Definitely not in the last fortnight.'

'Did he have problems with his eyes?'

'Not in his room. He never wore his sunglasses when he was in here, but he put them on to go to the toilet, which is at the end of the corridor.'

'In other words, he was hiding?'

'I think so.'

'Did he seem scared?'

'I got that feeling. When I knocked on the door, I'd hear him start, and I had to say my name before he'd draw the bolt.'

'Was she scared too?'

'It wasn't the same with her. Until Monday.'

Her breast was out again, pale and limp.

'Or more exactly, until Tuesday morning. It was on Tuesday that I realized Perkins wasn't around anymore.'

'Did she tell you that he'd gone on a trip?'

'She didn't tell me anything. She was a different person. She asked me more than once to go and buy her some bread and meat. This evening . . .'

'Did you post the express letter?'

'Yes. She rang for me. I did all her little errands, and she tipped me well. I used to buy her the newspapers too.'

'Did you take up this evening's paper?'

'Yes.'

'Did she seem as if she was planning to go out?'

'No. She wasn't dressed.'

'What about when she gave you the letter?'

'She was wearing a housecoat. Here, this one hanging on the hook.'

'What time did you go to bed?'

'At nine. I start my shift at seven in the morning. I shine the shoes on three floors.'

'Thank you, Lucile. If you remember any little detail, call me at Quai des Orfèvres. If I'm not there, give a message to the inspector who answers.'

'Yes, Monsieur Maigret.'

'You can go to bed.'

She hovered around him for another moment, then smiled and murmured:

'Goodnight, Monsieur Maigret.'

'Goodnight, Lucile.'

He went downstairs a few minutes later and found the night porter waiting for him with a bottle of red wine at his elbow.

'Well, what did the landlady tell you?'

'She was very pleasant,' said Maigret. 'So was Lucile.'

'Did Lucile flirt with you?'

A habit of the chambermaid, presumably.

'Do you start your shift every evening at nine?'

'Yes. But I never get into bed before eleven, or even a little later, when the Folies-Bergère close up.'

'Did you get a good look at the man who picked up Madame Perkins this evening?'

'Only through the curtain, but enough of one.'

'Describe him to me.'

'A tall guy, blond hair, with a fedora tilted back on his head. He wasn't wearing an overcoat: that's what I noticed most because it's cold at the moment.'

'Perhaps his car was at the door?'

'No. I heard them walk off down the pavement.'

Maigret had the feeling this business with the overcoat reminded him of something, but he couldn't immediately think what.

'Did she seem to be going with him willingly?'

'What do you mean?'

'Did she open the door of the office?'

'She had to give me the key.'

'Did the man stay in the corridor?'

'Yes.'

'Did he seem to be threatening her?'

'He was quietly smoking a cigarette.'

'Did she leave any messages?'

'Nothing. She just handed me her key, saying, "Good evening, Jean." That was all.'

'Did you notice how she was dressed?'

'She was wearing a darkish coat and some sort of a grey hat.'

'Did she have any luggage?'

'No.'

'When her husband went out in the evenings, did he ever take a car?'

'I always saw him leave and come back on foot.'

'Did he go far?'

'I don't think so. He was never gone for much more than an hour.'

'Did they sometimes go out together?'

'At first.'

'Not in the last fortnight?'

'I don't think so, no.'

'Did he always have his sunglasses on?'

'Yes.'

Room 47 and the one next to it both gave on to the street. If the wife didn't go out with the man professing to be called Perkins, did that mean she was watching to make sure the coast was clear? Perhaps they had a signal when he got back telling him whether it was safe to come in?

The description of Perkins, clothes aside, resembled that of Mascarelli, known as Sloppy Joe.

Wouldn't the fact that he had disappeared on Monday night point to him being the unknown stranger who had been dumped out of a car on to the pavement on Rue Fléchier, almost at poor old Lognon's feet?

Maigret produced a photograph of Bill Larner from his pocket and showed it to the porter.

'Do you recognize this man?'

'I've never seen him.'

'Are you sure he didn't come and get Madame Perkins?'

'I'm certain.'

He showed him the other two photos, of Charlie and Cicero.

'What about these men?'

'Don't know them. I saw their photos this evening in the newspaper.'

Maigret had taken a taxi but hadn't asked it to wait. He started walking towards Faubourg Montmartre, hoping to find a cab, but he hadn't gone a hundred metres before he had the feeling he was being followed.

He stopped, and the sound of footsteps some distance behind immediately died away. He set off and the steps rang out again. He span around, and someone over fifty metres away turned around as well.

He could only make out a vague outline in the shadow of the buildings. He obviously couldn't start running. He couldn't call out to the stranger either.

At Faubourg Montmartre he ignored the passing taxis and went into an all-night bar, where a couple of women were waiting not particularly hopefully at the bar.

Convinced the stranger was lying in wait for him outside, he ordered a quick drink and made for the telephone booth.

6.

Where everyone starts playing rough, and bones get broken

The third district police station was only a few buildings away from the harshly lit bar Maigret had gone into. If Lognon hadn't been so keen, it would have taken on the case, since Rue Fléchier, where the body had been dumped, was on the edge of its patch.

Maigret dialled the station's number with a worried look on his face.

'Hello? Who's that? It's Maigret speaking.'

'Inspector Bonfils, sir.'

'How many men have you got with you, Bonfils?'

'Only two: big Nicolas and Danvers.'

'Listen carefully. I'm in the Bar du Soleil. A guy's tailing me.'

'What does he look like?'

'I've no idea. He's making sure to stay in the shadows and keep enough of a distance so that I can only see his silhouette.'

'Do you want us to take him in for questioning?'

Maigret almost snapped, like Pozzo and Luigi: 'He's not an amateur!'

'Listen carefully,' he said. 'If the guy has come up to the window and seen me go into the phone booth, he'll have realized what I'm doing and, in that case, he's probably making himself scarce as we speak. If he hasn't seen me, he will have still considered the possibility of my telephoning and . . . What's that?'

'I was saying that people don't think of everything.'

'*Most people* don't, I know. At any event, he is on his guard.'

Although he couldn't see Bonfils' face, Maigret was sure it bore a mildly ironic expression. What a fuss about simply accosting some unsuspecting guy in the street! It was completely standard. They did it ten times a day.

'Are you staying in the bar, chief?'

'No. There are still people out and about. I'd rather we did it in a deserted street. Rue Grange-Batelière will do. It's not long and it will be easy to seal it off at both ends. Send two or three uniformed men to Rue Drouot right away and tell them not to show themselves and to have their guns at the ready.'

'Is it as serious as that?'

'Probably. Nicolas and Danvers are to take up position on the steps of Passage Jouffroy. I suppose the gates to the alley are locked now?'

'Yes.'

'Go over their instructions with them at least twice. In about ten minutes, I'll leave the bar and make my way slowly towards Rue Grange-Batelière. As I pass the entrance to the alley, your men should stay put. Then, when the man who's following me gets to them, they jump him. But be careful! He'll be armed.'

Knowing he was making the inspector smile, Maigret added:

'Unless I'm very much mistaken, he's a killer. Meanwhile I want you to take a few men and seal off Rue du Faubourg-Montmartre.'

It was unusual to use such numbers to arrest one man, but even so, at the last minute Maigret had another thought.

'To be doubly sure, put a car in Rue Drouot.'

'Talking of cars, chief . . .'

'What is it?'

'It's probably irrelevant, but I'll tell you anyway, just in case. Has the man been following you for long?'

'Since Rue Richer.'

'Do you know how he got there?'

'No.'

'About half an hour ago, one of our men found a stolen car in Faubourg Montmartre, actually just up from Rue Richer. The description was put out at the start of the afternoon.'

'Where was it stolen?'

'Porte Maillot.'

'Has it been towed?'

'No. It's still in the same place.'

'Don't touch it. Now, repeat the instructions.'

Bonfils repeated them like a model student, even the word 'killer', which he stumbled over slightly.

'Will ten minutes be enough?'

'Let's say fifteen.'

'I'll leave the bar in fifteen minutes. Everyone armed.'

He wasn't armed himself. He headed to the counter, where he drank a hot toddy for his worsening cold, with his back turned to the girls, who were looking optimistically in his direction.

Now and then a couple passed by outside. It was one in the morning, and most of the taxis were heading to nightclubs in Montmartre. Maigret drank another hot toddy with his eyes fixed on the clock, then buttoned up his overcoat, opened the door and, jamming his hands in his pockets, started walking. He was going back the way he had come, so the man following him should have been up ahead, but he couldn't see anyone. Had he walked past the bar while he was in the telephone booth?

He avoided turning round, to have the element of surprise on his side. He kept up a steady pace, even stopping under a streetlight and pretending to look something up in his address book.

The stolen car was still by the side of the road without a policeman in sight. In all there must have been about ten passers-by in the street, and you could hear the piercing voices of a group who seemed to have been drinking heavily.

Maigret would only know if he was still being followed when he got to Rue Grange-Batelière, and his chest was a little tight as he turned into it. He had gone fifty metres when he thought he heard footsteps rounding the corner of the street.

Now it was almost all down to big Nicolas, a giant of a man who liked nothing better than a scrap. Maigret didn't look round as he passed Passage Jouffroy, but he knew there were two figures on the steps leading from the pavement to the locked alley. In the hotel opposite, lights were still on in two or three windows.

He carried on walking, smoking his pipe, calculating that the man was about to draw level with the passage. Another dozen steps . . .

Now, he must be there . . .

Maigret was expecting the sound of a struggle, of bodies rolling on the cobbles maybe. But what stopped him in his tracks was a gunshot out of the blue.

He turned and saw a short, stocky man in the middle of the street firing a second time in the direction of the passage, then a third.

A whistle blew on the corner of Faubourg Montmartre: it must be Bonfils alerting his men.

Rue Grange-Batelière was guarded at both ends. A body had slumped forwards from the steps – probably Nicolas', because it looked enormous stretched out on the pavement. Now the other policeman, Danvers, was firing. The men on the corner of Rue Drouot came running, one of them firing far too early and almost hitting Maigret. Then the police car began moving in.

The killer's chances of escaping were all but nil, but events took a miraculous turn thanks to an incredible coincidence.

Just as the policemen were closing in from both sides, a vegetable truck bound for Les Halles turned the corner of Rue Drouot, heading for some unfathomable reason towards Faubourg Montmartre. It was driving fast, making a deafening racket. The driver couldn't work out what was going on around him. He must have heard the shooting.

One of the policemen shouted something at him, probably telling him to stop, but instead the frightened driver accelerated hard and shot down the street.

The stranger seized his chance and jumped on the back of the lorry, as Danvers blazed away and Nicolas, from where he was lying on the pavement, kept firing too.

The police still seemed to have the upper hand, given that the squad car was in pursuit, but the car hadn't reached the corner of Faubourg Montmartre before one of its tyres was hit by a bullet and burst.

Bonfils, who had jumped out of the way as the truck passed, whistled even louder to alert whoever might be on duty on the corner of the Grands Boulevards. But they hadn't been briefed. They just saw a truck going past and wondered what they were supposed to do.

Some passers-by had panicked and started running when they heard the shooting.

Maigret knew the game was up at that point. Leaving it to Bonfils to give chase, he went over to big Nicolas and bent down to him.

'Wounded?'

'Right in the stomach,' Nicolas grunted, his face contorted.

The local station's van arrived. A stretcher was taken out.

'You know, chief, I'm sure I got him too,' said Nicolas, as he was lifted into the vehicle.

He was right. When they shone an electric torch on the cobbles in the middle of the street, where the gangster had been standing during the fight, they found bloodstains.

In the distance two or three further shots could be heard on the other side of the Grands Boulevards, over towards Les Halles. The man would have plenty of opportunities to get away round there. At this time lorries would be arriving from all parts of the countryside and starting to unload fruit and vegetables in the middle of the street. The whole neighbourhood would be jammed. Hundreds of down-and-outs would be waiting for the chance to earn a bit of money for some manual labour, and drunks would be spilling out of seedy bars.

Head bowed, Maigret made for the police station and went into Bonfils' empty office. There was a little stove in the middle of the room, and he automatically started refilling it.

The station was almost empty. There was only a sergeant and three police officers, who didn't dare ask him any questions, their attitude one of stunned amazement.

This wasn't the usual way of things. It had all happened too quickly; matter-of-fact and brutal, the gunfight had completely unnerved them.

'Have you told the Police Emergency Services?' Maigret asked the sergeant.

'The minute I found out. They are cordoning off Les Halles.'

Standard procedure. Not that it would do any good. If the man had managed to escape half a dozen armed men in a deserted street guarded at both ends, he wouldn't have any trouble vanishing into the milling crowds of Les Halles.

'Don't you expect anything to come of it?'

'Where have they taken Nicolas?'

'To Hôtel-Dieu.'

'I'm going to Quai des Orfèvres. Keep me informed.'

He took a taxi and, crossing Les Halles, was stopped twice by roadblocks. A massive round-up was underway. Girls were running in every direction to escape the police. The prison van was parked near one of the halls.

Maigret had known from the start that Pozzo and Luigi weren't that far off the mark. Cinaglia and Co. weren't amateurs or beginners. They almost seemed to be guessing the police's every move and acting accordingly.

He slowly climbed the great staircase and went through the inspectors' room, where Vacher, who didn't know the latest yet, was making coffee on a portable stove.

'Do you want some, chief?'

'Please.'

'Did you find the Mado you were looking for?'

After a glance at Maigret, he didn't press the point.

Maigret had taken off his overcoat. Without realizing, he had sat down at his desk with his hat still on and automatically started fiddling with a pencil.

He dialled his home number distractedly and heard his wife's voice say:

'Is that you?'

'I probably won't be home tonight.'

'What's the matter?'

'Nothing.'

'You seem out of sorts. Is it your cold?'

'Maybe.'

'Is anything wrong?'

'Goodnight.'

Vacher brought him a steaming cup of coffee, and he went and opened a cupboard where he always kept a bottle of brandy in reserve.

'Do you want some?'

'A drop in my coffee won't do any harm.'

'Has the Baron telephoned?'

'Not yet.'

'Have you got his private number?'

'I've got it written down.'

'Call him.'

That was another thing worrying him. Baron had promised to telephone, and it was unlikely he was still out on the trail at this hour.

'There's no answer, chief.'

'Lucas?'

'I sent him home to bed, as you told me to.'

'Torrence?'

'He followed the lady to the Folies-Bergère, then to a brasserie on Rue Royale, where she had dinner with a girl-friend. After that she went home on her own, and Janvier is still watching the building.'

Maigret shrugged. What was the point of any of it, when his adversary was always a step ahead? He gritted his teeth, thinking of Pozzo and his advice, of Luigi's patronizing attitude. The message in both cases seemed to be:

'You're a good soul, inspector, and when you're up against the second-rate criminals you get here in Paris, you're one of the best. But this business isn't for you. These guys play rough and they may hurt you. Just drop it! What concern is it of yours, anyway?'

He telephoned Hôtel-Dieu and had a difficult time being put through to a member of staff who could tell him what was going on.

'They're operating on him now,' he was told.

'Is it serious?'

'Laparotomy.'

First they had taken Lognon to Saint-Germain forest, battered him about the face and knocked him unconscious with the butt of a pistol! Now they had shot Big Nicolas right in the stomach before he had even had time to move!

Which meant that, while he was following Maigret along Rue Grange-Batelière, the man was expecting a trap and had his gun in his hand, ready to shoot. It was a miracle that Danvers hadn't been hit as well.

Judging by his silhouette, it was Charlie. And Charlie, who barely knew Paris and didn't speak a word of French, had still nearly carried out a hit single-handed, right in the heart of town.

Mascarelli, or Sloppy Joe, as he was nicknamed, had left Montreal under a false name with a woman who was apparently not his lover.

The other two, Charlie and Cicero, had embarked in New York under their real names. They had made no attempt to hide, as though they had nothing to fear, then registered under their real names in a hotel in Rue de l'Étoile.

Did they already know what they were after? Probably. They also knew who to turn to for help.

Maigret would have sworn that a man like Bill Larner, who had never used strong-arm methods, wasn't exactly happy to cooperate with them.

But, one way or another, they had collared him and sent him to a garage to hire a car.

Had they known Mascarelli's address when they landed? It wasn't definite, since they had waited nearly two weeks to attack him.

They didn't do anything rashly, coldly stacking all the odds in their favour.

In the two weeks they had spent preparing, they had probably eaten regularly at Pozzo's with Larner.

Had they also gone to the Manhattan? Possibly. Honest citizen though he was, Luigi wouldn't have said anything to Maigret.

Hadn't he made a point of talking about those American shopkeepers who would rather pay a ransom to the racketeers than take a bullet?

Meanwhile Sloppy Joe seemed to know what was up because for the last fortnight – in other words, ever since the other two had landed – he had taken twice as many precautions.

It was a poker game where lives were at stake, and everyone seemed to be able to see their opponent's cards.

Knowing he was in danger, Sloppy Joe lay low in his hotel on Rue Richer, only venturing out for a few minutes in the evening in sunglasses, like a movie star.

Charlie and Cicero must have been watching him for several days, readying their trap. On Monday evening, in the car hired by Larner, they had lain in wait near the Hôtel de Bretagne.

It must have happened exactly as with Lognon: the car pulling up by the side of the road, the gun pointed at Mascarelli . . .

'Get in!'

In the heart of town, when the streets were still busy.

Had they taken him out to the country before shooting him? Probably not. Chances were they had used a gun with a silencer. Moments later, they had tipped the body out on to the pavement of Rue Fléchier.

Maigret drew little figures on a piece of paper like a schoolboy doodling in the margins of his exercise book.

As the car was pulling away, either Charlie or Cicero had seen Lognon's silhouette. No doubt it was too late to shoot. Besides, it didn't matter at that point whether the body was found or not because the job was done.

Maigret was sure he was right about all of this. The car would have driven round the neighbourhood and come back down Rue Fléchier a few moments later, and the men would have seen that the body had been removed. The police couldn't have done it; they would have taken longer and had formalities to observe. But there was no one in sight.

How were they going to find out who had taken it away?

'They're professionals,' Luigi had stressed.

And that's how they had behaved. Suspecting that the man they had glimpsed had taken down their licence number, they were waiting the following day outside the garage that had rented them the car. Then they had followed Lognon, probably expecting to find the dead or injured man at his home.

Charlie and Cicero, who didn't speak a word of French, couldn't question the concierge or Madame Lognon.

So they sent Larner instead.

Their faces must have been a picture when they discovered that the man in Rue Fléchier was none other than a police inspector. Talking of which, they must have thought: why wasn't there anything in the newspapers about the affair either?

Obviously it was vital for them to find their victim, dead or alive. But equally, now that they knew that the police were on their trail, they had to drop out of sight.

Since then they seemed to have anticipated and thwarted Maigret's every last move.

They left their various hotels and then, when Pozzo called, they abandoned their hiding place on Rue Brunel.

The three men's photographs appeared in the newspapers.

Within a few hours, Sloppy Joe's travelling companion had disappeared from her hotel. And when Maigret left that same hotel, he was tailed by Charlie Cinaglia, who had no compunction starting a Chicago-style shoot-out in Rue Grange-Batelière.

'Vacher!'

'Yes, chief . . .'

'Will you make sure the Baron hasn't gone home?'

This business with the Baron was making him increasingly anxious. The inspector had told him he was going to nose around a few bars that were popular with the racing fraternity.

Maigret didn't underestimate his opponent. Baron might learn something, but while he was doing so, wouldn't the others realize that he was on their trail? Wouldn't he find himself in the same situation as Lognon?

'Still no answer.'

'You're sure you've got the right number?'

'I'll check.'

Vacher called the switchboard operator and made sure he wasn't mistaken.

'What time is it?'

'Five to two.'

It had just occurred to him that the Manhattan was one of the town's real racing bars. Perhaps it was still open? If not, Luigi might still be cashing up.

As he had anticipated, Luigi answered the telephone.

'Maigret here.'

'Oh.'

'Is your place still busy?'

'I closed ten minutes ago. I'm alone in the bar. I was just about to leave.'

'Tell me, Luigi, do you know an inspector who's known as the Baron?'

'The racing guy?'

'Yes. I'd like to know if you've seen him this evening.'

'I have.'

'What time?'

'Wait, there were still a lot of people in the bar. It must have been around eleven thirty. It was just after the theatres came out.'

'Did he talk to you?'

'Not personally.'

'Do you know who he talked to?'

There was a silence at the end of the line.

'Listen, Luigi. You're a decent guy, and there's never been anything against you.'

'So?'

'One of my inspectors has just been shot in the stomach.'

'Is he dead?'

'They're operating on him at the moment. A woman has been abducted from her hotel room.'

'Do you know who she is?'

'Sloppy Joe's girl.'

Another silence.

'The Baron didn't go to your place just to have a drink.'

'I'm listening.'

'Charlie shot my inspector.'

'Have you arrested him?'

'He managed to get away, but he was hit.'

'What do you want to know?'

'I haven't heard from the Baron and I need to find him.'

'How am I supposed to know where he's gone?'

'Perhaps if you tell me who he talked to this evening, that will give me a lead.'

Another silence, longer than before.

'Listen, inspector. I think you'd better come and have a chat with me. I'm not sure it will really be worth it, because I don't know very much. Actually, thinking about it, it's best we don't meet here. You never know.'

'Will you come by my office?'

'Not there either, but thanks. Wait a moment – if you want to go to La Coupole on Boulevard Montparnasse and make sure you're not followed, I'll meet you there in the bar.'

'How soon?'

'The time it takes to lock up and get there. My car's at the door.'

Before he left, Maigret telephoned the hospital again.

'There's a chance we can save him,' he was told.

Then he got Bonfils on the telephone.

'Did you catch him?'

'No. Half an hour ago they came to tell us that a car had been stolen on Rue de la Victoire. I've circulated its licence number.'

Always the same methods.

'By the way, Bonfils, did you have a look at the other car that was dumped on Faubourg Montmartre?'

'I had the same thought. It was in the country today because it's still streaked with wet mud. I telephoned its owner, who told me that it was clean this morning.'

Downstairs Maigret took a Préfecture car, whose driver he had to wake up.

'La Coupole.'

Luigi, who had got there before him, was having a couple of sausages and a glass of beer at a little table by the bar. The place was virtually empty.

'Were you followed?'

'No.'

'Take a seat. What are you having?'

'The same.'

This was the first time Maigret had seen Luigi outside his establishment. He was serious, worried. He started speaking in a low voice without taking his eyes off the door.

'I don't like – and I mean, I really don't like – getting involved in things like this. But then again, if I don't, I'll have you on my back.'

'You will,' Maigret said coldly.

'I tried to warn you this morning. Now it looks as if it's too late.'

'The curtain's gone up, that's right, and it won't come down until the show's over. What do you know?'

'Nothing definite. It may get you somewhere, though. Any other evening, I probably wouldn't have paid any attention to the Baron. But I noticed him tonight because that made it the second . . .'

He seemed to be trying to bite his tongue, so Maigret muttered:

'. . . the second cop of the day.'

He added:

'Had the Baron been drinking?'

'He wasn't on water.'

It was one of the inspector's failings, but he rarely lost his head.

'He sat on his own in a corner for quite a long time, watching the customers, then he went to talk to someone called Loris, who used to be a trainer for one of the Rothschilds. I don't know what they talked about. Loris likes a drink. It cost him his job, in fact. They were at the far end of the bar, by the wall. Then I saw them go over to one of the tables at the back, where Loris introduced the Baron to Bob.'

'Who's Bob?'

'A jockey.'

'American?'

'He lived in Los Angeles for a long time, but I don't think he's American.'

'Does he live in Paris?'

'Maisons-Laffitte.'

'Is that all?'

'Bob went to make a couple of telephone calls. They can't have been local calls, because he asked me for a fair few tokens.'

'As if he was ringing Maisons-Laffitte?'

'Pretty much.'

'Did they leave together?'

'No. I lost sight of them for a while because, as I said, it was the rush after the theatres came out. When I looked at their table again, Bob and your friend were on their own.'

Maigret couldn't remotely see where this was getting them. Luigi signalled to the waiter to bring them two more glasses of beer.

'There was a customer at the bar who was watching them,' Luigi then said.

'Who?'

'A lad who's been dropping in for the odd whiskey for the past few days. Actually he was in this morning when you were at the bar.'

'A tall guy with blond hair?'

'He told me to call him Harry. All I know is that he's from St Louis.'

'Like Charlie and Cicero,' muttered Maigret.

'Exactly.'

'Did he talk to you about them?'

'He didn't ask me any questions. The first day he stopped for a moment in front of the photo of Charlie in his boxing days and there was a strange smile on his face.'

'Could he hear what Bob and the Baron were saying?'

'No. He just watched them.'

'Did he follow them when they left?'

'We haven't got to that yet. Don't forget that I'm only telling you what I saw, I'm not drawing any conclusions. It's still far too much, though, I'm sorry to say, and I'd be much happier if Charlie was dead rather than just wounded. Bob came to ask me if I'd seen Billy Fast.'

'Who's Billy Fast?'

'A sort of bookmaker who also lives somewhere in Maisons-Laffitte. He was in the basement. I don't know if you've been down there before. Below the bar there's a sort of little lounge where the regulars go.'

'I know it.'

'Bob went down first on his own. Then he came and got your inspector, and I didn't see them for a long time. Finally, at twelve fifteen at least, the Baron came through the bar, heading for the door.'

'On his own?'

'On his own. He was drunk.'

'Very?'

'No, but enough.'

'What about your customer from the bar, the tall guy with blond hair from St Louis?'

'That's just it. He left straight after him.'

Maigret thought that was his lot and stared gloomily at his glass. It obviously meant something, what he had just heard, but it was going to be a hell of a job working out what.

'Is that truthfully all you know?'

Luigi looked him in the face for a long time before replying:

'Do you realize I could be risking my neck?'

Maigret thought it best to keep quiet and wait.

'Of course it's understood that I haven't told you anything, that I didn't see you this evening, and that you are never, under any circumstances, going to call on my evidence.'

'I promise.'

'Billy Fast doesn't live in Maisons-Laffitte itself, but more often than not in a guesthouse in the forest.

I've heard him talk about it once or twice. As far as I can tell it's a place where a certain type of person goes to rest up from time to time. It's called Au Bon Vivant.'

'Is it run by an American?'

'By an American woman who used to be in a showgirl troupe and has got a soft spot for Billy.'

As Maigret went to take his wallet out of his pocket, Luigi waved him away and, with a scowling attempt at a smile, said:

'No, this is on me! Next thing they'll be saying I let the police stand me a drink. How much is it, waiter?'

They were each as worried as the other.

7.

In which it's Maigret's turn to go on the attack and he risks getting into some serious trouble

When Vacher saw Maigret come into his office, he knew immediately that there had been a new development, but realized that now wasn't the time to ask questions.

'Bonfils telephoned a few minutes ago,' he said. 'The man got through the roadblocks. A trader from Les Halles says she saw him hiding behind a stack of baskets and that he threatened her with his gun so she'd keep her mouth shut. This rings true because we found traces of blood on one of the baskets. In Rue Rambuteau, he bumped into a prostitute. According to her, he had one shoulder higher than the other. Bonfils thinks that rather than try to leave the area immediately, he stayed there for a while, changing places to keep ahead of the police. We're still patrolling round there.'

Maigret, who appeared not to be listening, had taken an automatic pistol out of his drawer and was checking the magazine.

'Do you know if Torrence is armed?'

'Probably not, unless you told him specially.'

Torrence liked to say his fists were a match for any weapon.

'Get me Lucas on the telephone.'

'You only sent him home to bed two hours ago.'

'I remember.'

Maigret's stare was hard, and he spoke in a drawl as if he was tired.

'Is that you, Lucas? Sorry to wake you, my friend. I thought you wouldn't be happy if we saw it through tonight and you weren't around.'

'I'm coming, chief.'

'Not here. You'll save time if you jump in a car and get it to drive you to Avenue de la Grande-Armée, on the corner of Rue Brunel. I've got to pick up Torrence from there. By the way, bring your gun.'

After a pause, Lucas objected:

'What about Janvier?'

There were only a few people in the Police Judiciaire who would have understood this question. Even before the chief mentioned a gun, Lucas had realized this was serious. Maigret was ringing him in person, and he was going to relieve Torrence from his stakeout so he could take him along too. So Lucas automatically thought of Janvier, the other trusted member of the inner circle, as if an expedition without him made no sense.

'Janvier is at home. It would take too long to go and fetch him.'

He lived in the suburbs, in the opposite direction to where they were going.

'Can't I come along?' Vacher asked shyly.

'Who'd stay on duty?'

'Buchet's in his office.'

'We can't leave him in charge of everything. Do you know Maisons-Laffitte?'

'I've often driven through it. I've been to the races there a couple of times.'

'Do you know the country around there, by the forest?'

'I used to go there too in the old days, with the kids.'

'Have you heard of a place called Au Bon Vivant?'

'There are bistros called that all over the place. The easiest thing would be to ring the gendarmerie. Shall I call them?'

'That's the last thing you should do! Don't call the local police either. Or anyone at all. Don't even mention Maisons-Laffitte. Do you understand?'

'Yes, chief.'

'Goodnight, then, Vacher.'

'Goodnight, chief.'

Maigret had hesitated, glancing at the cupboard where the bottle of brandy was kept, but his pockets were weighed down with the two revolvers as it was. Downstairs, he asked the officer driving the car:

'Are you armed?'

'Yes, sir.'

'Do you have children?'

'I'm only twenty-three.'

'That shouldn't stop you.'

'I'm not married.'

He was one of the new breed of policeman, more like an Olympic champion than one of the paunchy, mustachioed officers you used to see on street corners.

A fairly strong, very cold wind had got up, giving the night an odd character. Two distinct layers of cloud were visible in the sky. The lower one, a mass of thick, dark clouds moving very fast before the wind, ensured it was pitch black for most of the time. But occasionally it would split open, and they could see, as though through a cleft between rocks, a lunar landscape where very high, fleecy, glittering clouds stood motionless.

'Don't drive too fast.'

They had to allow Lucas, who lived on the Left Bank, time to get to Avenue de la Grande-Armée. Maigret had debated whether to accept Vacher's offer. For a moment he had even thought of taking Bonfils, who would have been delighted.

He was aware of the responsibility he was assuming, and of just how much trouble he could be getting into. For a start he had no authority to operate in Maisons-Laffitte, which was outside his jurisdiction. By rights he should have referred the matter to Rue des Saussaies, which would have sent men from the Sûreté Nationale, or got a rogatory commission for the Seine-et-Oise gendarmerie, which would have taken hours.

Prudence alone seemed to dictate a heavy police presence, given what he knew of his adversary and what had just happened on Rue Richer. But Maigret was convinced that would be asking for a fight.

That was why he had chosen Torrence and Lucas. He would have brought along Janvier too if he could, and maybe, to give him an opportunity, young Lapointe.

'Turn into Rue Brunel. Stop when you see Torrence.'

There he was, stamping his feet.

'Get in. Are you armed?'

'No, chief. You know, the girl's not dangerous.'

Maigret gave him one of the two revolvers as the car drew up at the corner of the avenue.

'Have you had a tip-off? Are we going to arrest them?'

'Probably.'

'If I'd been a soft touch back there, you wouldn't have found me.'

'Why's that?'

'Because I would have been in the young lady's bed. She was already at it when she left for the theatre, coming up to me and saying, "Why don't you come in my taxi?" I didn't see any reason why not, and she rubbed her thigh against mine. "Aren't you coming to see the show?" I chose to stand guard outside her dressing room. We came back together.'

'Did she talk at all?'

'Only about Bill Larner. She really doesn't seem to know the other two and she swore to me that she was afraid of them. She took a girlfriend to Rue Royale to have something to eat. She invited me as well, but I refused. Then we came back here on our own and stayed out on the doorstep for ages like lovers.

'"You don't think you'd keep a closer eye on me if you came upstairs?" she asked.

'I knew what she was saying. What would you have done in my place? Mind you, I wouldn't have objected . . .'

Maigret suspected Torrence was chattering away on purpose to release some of his tension. A taxi stopped just behind the police car, a door slammed, then Lucas came towards them with a jaunty spring in his step.

'Shall we be off?' he asked.

'You didn't forget your gun, did you?' Maigret asked, then said to the driver:

'Maisons-Laffitte.'

They drove through Neuilly and Courbevoie. It was three thirty in the morning, and there were still lorries heading towards Les Halles – heavy goods vehicles, overnight deliveries – but hardly any cars.

'Do you know where they're hiding out, chief?'

'Maybe. It's not definite. The Baron hasn't called me back as he promised to. I'm afraid he might have had the same bright idea as Lognon and decided to work alone.'

'Has he been drinking?'

'Apparently.'

'Did he have his car?'

Maigret frowned.

'Has he got a car?'

'He's had one for about a fortnight, a convertible he bought second-hand. He drives around everywhere.'

Didn't that explain the inspector's silence? When he left Luigi's bar, after a few too many drinks, and found his car at the door, wouldn't he have wanted to take a spin out to Maisons-Laffitte to check his lead?

It was Lucas who asked:

'Have you called the gendarmerie?'

Maigret shook his head.

'Does Rue des Saussaies know?'

'I didn't do that either.'

They understood one another. For a while, there was a weighty silence.

'Are there still three of them?'

'Unless they've split up, which I don't think they have. Charlie's wounded. As far as we can tell, he's been hit in the shoulder.'

Maigret gave a brief summary of the Rue Richer affair, to which they listened in knowledgeable silence.

'He seems to have come to Paris on his own. Do you think he went to get the woman?'

'It looks that way. Apparently he was too late.'

'If he planned to do the job without his pals, he can't have thought it would be that difficult.'

They were each as uneasy as the other, because they didn't feel on familiar ground. Usually, on a case, they could accurately predict how their adversary would react. They knew virtually the full range of criminals.

But these ones' methods threw them. They acted faster. In fact the speed with which they made decisions seemed their main characteristic. At the same time, they didn't think twice about showing themselves, as if the fact the police knew their identities and their every move struck them as irrelevant.

'Do we shoot?' asked Torrence.

'If there's no alternative. I wouldn't want someone to die on me.'

'Do you have an idea how we're going to play it?'

'No.'

All he knew was that he'd had enough of it all and he wanted to put a stop to it one way or another. These people had crossed the Atlantic and killed a man in the centre of Paris, then given Lognon a beating and fired point-blank at a police officer, not to mention abducted a woman opposite the Folies-Bergère.

Despite their photographs being in all the newspapers, despite every police force having their descriptions, they were moving around a city they barely knew as if they were at home, stealing random cars whenever they needed them as easily as hailing a taxi.

'What shall I do?' asked the driver, as they crossed the bridge and saw the lights of Maisons-Laffitte.

They made out the chateau, the pale splash of the race-track in the moonlight. The streets were deserted, with only the odd light in a window now and then. They needed to find the Bon Vivant and, as they were driving past the blue light of the police station, the easiest way obviously would be to ask in there.

'Keep going. There's a level crossing a little further on.'

Luckily there was a light on in the level-crossing keeper's hut. A train must have been due any moment. Maigret got out of the car, went into the hut and found a man with a bushy moustache alone with a bottle of wine.

'Do you know a guesthouse called the Bon Vivant?'

Endless explanations followed. Unable to make head or tail of the crossroads and left and right turns the man was listing, Maigret had to call the driver.

'You take the second level crossing and head towards l'Étoile-des-Tetrons. You know the one I mean? Whatever you do, don't take the road to Château de la Muette, but the one just before it . . .'

The driver seemed to understand. Nevertheless, ten minutes later they were lost in the forest and had to get out at each crossroads to decipher the names on the sign-posts. The clouds had closed over again, and they had to use a flashlight.

'There's a car parked in front of us with all its lights off.'

'We'd better go and have a look.'

It was parked in the middle of the road in the heart of the forest. The four of them started walking, as Maigret told them to draw their guns. It was a side road, and dead leaves rustled at their every step.

Such precautions may have been absurd, but Maigret didn't want to put his men's lives in danger, and it took them almost ten minutes to close in on the abandoned car.

It was empty. The nameplate inside bore the name of a manufacturer and an address on Rue de Rivoli. The flash-light, pointed at the driver's seat, showed bloodstains, still wet. Another stolen car!

'Can you understand why he left it here? There isn't a house in sight. If we are where I think we are and the level-crossing keeper wasn't mistaken, the Bon Vivant is at least half a kilometre away.'

'Do you want to check the petrol, Lucas?'

That was it, the most simple, banal explanation imaginable. Charlie had grabbed the first car he had come across and suddenly run out of petrol. The car interior still smelled of cigarettes.

'Let's go! They mustn't hear us.'

'Do you think the Baron came this way?'

The road was muddy in places, but the dead leaves were too thick to make out footprints or tyre tracks. Besides, they had to be careful not to use their flashlights now.

They finally reached a bend, beyond which stretched a clearing to the left. In the clearing they saw lights feebly gleaming from behind two curtained windows. Maigret whispered his instructions:

'You,' he said to the driver, 'stay here and only go closer if there's fighting. Torrence, you go round to the back of the house in case they try to get out that way.'

'Shall I aim at their legs?'

'Ideally. Lucas will come with me near the shack, but will hang back a little to watch the windows.'

They were all intimidated, even though every one of them had carried out harder arrests. Maigret thought in particular of a Pole who had terrorized a series of farms in the north for months and ended up hiding out in a little hotel in Paris, armed to the teeth. He was another killer, someone who, if he felt you were on to him, could shoot into a crowd of people and wreak absolute carnage just so he could go out with a bang.

What was so exceptional about these men? It was as though Pozzo and Luigi had given Maigret some sort of complex.

'Good luck, boys!'

'Break a leg,' grunted Torrence, touching wood.

Lucas, who claimed not to be superstitious, repeated in an almost reluctant whisper, 'Break a leg!'

As far as they could judge, the Bon Vivant was a former gamekeeper's house with at most three rooms on the ground floor and the same number on the first. It had a pointed, slate-covered roof, which they could make out thanks to a shaft of moonlight.

Maigret and Lucas silently approached the lights on the ground floor. When they were only about twenty metres away, Maigret touched his inspector on the arm, indicating he should turn left.

Maigret himself waited a few minutes without moving, so as to be sure that everyone was in position. Luckily the wind, which was stronger here than in Paris, was shaking the tree branches and rustling the leaves on the ground. For about two minutes they were all at risk because a break in the clouds meant the moon was so bright that Maigret could see the buttons on Torrence's overcoat and Lucas' gun, even though he was further away from him than the house was. The minute the clouds closed over again he took his chance and crossed the space between him and one of the lit-up windows. It had red-checked curtains, like at Pozzo's, but they were clumsily drawn, and he could see inside through the gap between them.

He found himself looking at the main room, which had a zinc bar and half a dozen polished wooden tables. The whitewashed walls were covered with bad colour prints. There were no chairs in the room, just rustic benches, and on one of them Charlie Cinaglia was sitting with his profile to Maigret.

His chest was bare and flabby, and tufts of very dark hair stood out against his white skin. A large woman with bleached-blonde hair came out of the kitchen with a steaming saucepan. Her lips were moving. She was saying something, but her voice didn't carry outside.

Tony Cicero was there too, without a jacket. On the table, next to a bottle of what must have been pure alcohol or some sort of disinfectant, were two automatic pistols.

Looking at the floor, Maigret saw a basin of pinkish water with pieces of cotton wool floating in it.

Charlie was still bleeding, which seemed to worry him. The bullet had hit the tip of his left shoulder and without going in, as far as Maigret could tell, had torn off a piece of flesh.

None of the three individuals seemed to be on their guard. The woman poured some hot water into a saucer and added a little of the contents of the bottle. She dipped in a piece of cotton wool, then swabbed the wound as Charlie gritted his teeth.

Tony Cicero, cigar in mouth, grabbed a bottle of whiskey from one of the tables and handed it to his friend, who took a swig from the bottle. Bill Larner was nowhere in sight. Maigret wasn't able to see Cicero from the front at first, but when he did, he was surprised to see he had a black eye.

What followed was such a blur that no one knew exactly what was happening.

As he handed the bottle back to Cicero, Charlie looked over at the window. Maigret was presumably not as invisible from inside as he had thought because, without a feature of Charlie's face betraying that he was on the alert, he reached out with his good arm, and his hand closed on one of the two pistols.

At the same instant Maigret pulled the trigger of his pistol, and, just like in a Hollywood film, Charlie's gun tumbled to the ground as his hand dangled uselessly from his wrist.

Moving with equal speed, without turning round, Cicero had tipped over the table, which now shielded him. Taking a couple of steps, the woman pressed herself against the wall by the window, where she couldn't be hit.

Maigret ducked just in time as a bullet shattered one of the windowpanes, then another blew off part of the frame.

He heard footsteps to his left, Lucas', who came running.

'Did you get him?'

'I got one of them. Watch out!'

Cicero was still firing. Lucas got down on all fours and crawled to the door.

'What shall I do?' yelled the driver, whom they had left behind.

'Stay where you are.'

Maigret raised his head to try to see inside, and a bullet went through his hat.

He was wondering where Bill Larner was and whether he would join in. They had no idea where he might be, which made it even more dangerous. He could attack them on the flank, firing from one of the first-floor windows, say, or surprise them from behind.

Lucas kicked open the door.

As he did so, a voice inside let out a sort of war cry. It was Torrence, screaming:

'Go to it, chief!'

The woman was screaming too. Lucas ran in. Maigret straightened and saw two men fighting on the floor, on the other side of the overturned table, and the landlady grabbing an andiron in the fireplace.

Lucas got to her in time to stop her hitting Torrence, and it was funny seeing him, so tiny, pinioning the American woman, who was a head taller than him, by the wrists.

The next moment Maigret was in the room as well. On the floor, Charlie was trying to reach one of the revolvers which was only about twenty centimetres from his hand. Maigret did something he had never done in his entire career. For once, he furiously gave vent to his rage, crushing the hand of the killer under his heel.

'Dirty brute!' spat the woman, whom Lucas was still restraining. Torrence was pinning Cicero to the ground with his full weight, as the American tried to dig his fingers into his eyes, and Maigret had to make several attempts before he fitted handcuffs on him.

When Torrence got back to his feet, he was beaming. Dust from the floor had stuck to his sweaty face, and Cicero had torn the collar of his shirt and given him a nasty scratch on the cheek.

'Don't you want to put her in handcuffs too, chief?'

Lucas, completely worn out, asked for help, and Maigret ended up putting Torrence's handcuffs on the landlady of the Bon Vivant.

'Aren't you ashamed, manhandling a woman?'

The driver stood framed in the door.

'Do you need me?'

Lifting up Charlie, who was grimacing with pain, by the shoulders, Torrence asked:

'What shall I do with him, chief?'

'Sit him in a corner.'

'When I heard the shots, I decided to go in by the back. The door was closed. I broke a window and found myself in the kitchen.'

Maigret filled his pipe slowly, meticulously, as he caught his breath. Then he went over to a glass cabinet containing glasses.

'Who wants a whiskey?'

But he was still concerned, and he sent the driver out to make sure no one tried to escape from the house.

He said to Lucas:

'Do you want to go round and see there isn't another car?'

He glanced in the kitchen, where the remains of a cold supper lay on a table, and pushed open a door to a smaller room that must have been used as a dining room.

Then he started up the stairs, his revolver still warm in his hand. Stopping on the landing to listen, he pushed open another door with his foot.

'Anyone in there?'

There was no one. It was the landlady's room, its walls covered with photographs of men and women, like Pozzo's restaurant. There were at least a hundred pictures, many of them signed to Helen, and some of the photographs were of her, twenty years or so younger and dressed as a showgirl.

Before studying them Maigret made sure there wasn't anyone in the other two bedrooms. The beds hadn't been slept in. One of the rooms contained suitcases, in which Maigret found silk underwear, toiletries, shoes, but not a trace of any papers.

These were obviously the suitcases Charlie and Cicero had brought during their successive trips back and forth. At the very bottom of the heaviest one there were another two automatic pistols, a silencer, a cosh and a rubber truncheon, not to mention a sizeable supply of ammunition.

Of the woman who had travelled with Sloppy Joe, not a trace. Whereas, on his way back through the kitchen, Maigret picked up a cigarette case with the initials B. L. near the coffee pot, which seemed to suggest that Larner had been there.

Lucas returned from his inspection, his feet muddy.

'No car in the vicinity, chief.'

In the meantime Torrence had examined the wounded man's hand, which the bullet had gone through. Strangely, the wound wasn't bleeding, because the blood had clotted on both sides, but the fingers were swelling almost visibly and turning blue.

'Is there a telephone in the house?'

There was one behind the door.

'Call a doctor in Maisons-Laffitte, any one will do, but don't say we're the police. Best to say there's been an accident.'

Lucas gestured to say he'd see to it, and, for the first time, not without hesitation or a certain embarrassment, Maigret tested out his bad English in front of his men.

He spoke to Cicero, who was sitting on a bench, leaning against the wall.

'Where's Bill Larner?'

As he had expected, he didn't get an answer, just a contemptuous smile.

'Bill was here tonight. Did he give you a black eye?'

The smile vanished, but Cicero's teeth remained clenched.

'As you wish. You seem like a tough guy, but we've got some tough characters on this continent too.'

'I want to telephone my consul,' Cicero said finally.

'What could be easier. At this hour. And to tell him what, may I ask?'

'You decide. But you'd better take responsibility.'

'That's just what I am doing. Did you get through to the doctor, Lucas?'

'He'll be here in a quarter of an hour.'

'Did you get the impression he'd call the police at Maisons?'

'I don't think so. He didn't bat an eyelid.'

'I wouldn't be surprised if they threw some wild parties here. Do you want to call the Police Judiciaire to see if they've got any news of the Baron?'

This business with the Baron was still worrying him, as was the woman's disappearance from the Hôtel de Bretagne.

'While you're at it, ask Vacher to send us a second car. Everyone won't fit into ours.'

Then, turning to face Charlie, he said:

'Nothing to tell me?'

All he got in reply was one of the crudest insults in the English language, an allusion to the way his mother had conceived him.

'What's he saying?' Torrence asked.

'He's discreetly hinting at my parentage.'

'Vacher hasn't got any news about the Baron, chief. He just rang his number again a quarter of an hour ago. Apparently Bonfils called to report that a car has been stolen . . .'

'Rue de Rivoli?'

'Yes.'

'Did you tell him we'd found it?'

A car stopped at the door, and a youngish man opened it, a black bag in his hand, then recoiled at the sight of the chaotic state of the room, the revolvers on one of the tables, and finally the handcuffs.

'Come in, doctor. Take no notice. We're from the police and we've been having a talk with these gentlemen and this lady.'

'Doctor,' she began, 'tell the Maisons-Laffitte police, who know me, that these brutes . . .'

Maigret identified himself and pointed to Charlie in the corner, who was about to pass out.

'I'd like you to fix him up a bit so he can come back to Paris with us. He was injured in Paris first and then again during our discussion here.'

While he attended to Charlie, Maigret went around the house again, paying particular attention to the photographs in the landlady's bedroom. Then he emptied one of the suitcases and stuffed it with all the photographs he had taken off the wall and the papers he had found in a drawer: letters, bills and newspaper clippings. Finally, after carefully wrapping them, he put in the cigarette case and the glasses and cups they had been using.

When he went back into the main room, Charlie was looking groggy. The doctor explained:

'I thought it best to give him an injection to sedate him.'

'Is it serious?'

'He has lost a lot of blood. They may decide to give him a transfusion at the hospital. He's tough.'

Cinaglia could only muster a dazed stare.

'Anyone else I should see to?'

'You'll stay and have a drink, won't you?'

Maigret knew what he was doing.

To prevent the Maisons-Laffitte police or the gendarmerie finding out, he wanted to make sure the doctor didn't leave before the car he had requested from Vacher arrived.

'Have a seat, doctor. Have you had reason to come here before?'

'Several times. Isn't that so, Helen?'

He seemed to know her very well.

'But under different circumstances. Once, it was a jockey who had broken his leg and spent a month recuperating on the first floor. Another time I was called out in the middle of the night to attend to a gentleman who had drunk too much and was suffering heart failure. I also seem to remember a girl who got hit on the head by a bottle – an accident, I was told, one night when everyone was in a fairly high state of excitement.'

Finally the car arrived. Charlie had to be carried out, his legs trembling. Cicero walked disdainfully round to the back seat, his hands on his stomach, and got in without a word.

'Are you going to sit next to them, Torrence?'

Torrence felt gratified, in a small but well-deserved way, since he had done the bulk of the work.

'Pity it's not still light and Pozzo's isn't still open.'

Perhaps if it had been nine thirty in the morning instead of four thirty, Maigret would have yielded to his desire to pass by Rue des Acacias and ask Pozzo to have a look in the car.

'Drop Charlie off at Beaujon hospital on the way. Lognon will be pleased to know he's under the same roof. Take the other one to headquarters.'

Then he said to the woman, who, according to her papers, was called Helen Donahue:

'Let's go!'

She looked him in the eye without stirring.

'I said, let's go!'

'You won't make me budge. This is my home. You haven't got a warrant. I demand to speak to my consul too.'

'Of course. We'll discuss that later. Would you care to accompany us?'

'No.'

'Ready, Lucas?'

Both of them took hold of the woman, one on either side, and lifted her off her feet. The doctor, who couldn't help laughing at the scene, held the door open for them. Helen struggled so hard that Lucas lost his grip, and she sprawled on the ground. They had to call the driver over to help.

Finally they bundled her into the car as best they could, and Lucas got in next to her.

'To headquarters!' Maigret ordered.

After a hundred metres, he changed his mind.

'Are you very tired, Lucas?'

'Not too bad. Why?'

'I don't like leaving the place empty.'

'Right you are. I'll get out.'

Maigret went round to sit in the back of the car. Lighting his pipe, he inquired politely of his neighbour:

'The smoke isn't bothering you, is it?'

All he got in reply was the insult he had translated very approximately a little earlier.

8.

In which an inspector tries to remember what he has found out

Comfortably settled in his corner, his overcoat collar turned up, his eyes stinging from tiredness and his head cold, Maigret stared straight ahead, ignoring his neighbour. They had been driving for less than five minutes when Helen started talking – to herself, it sounded like – in short bursts.

'Some smart-alec policemen are going to be taught a lesson round here . . .'

A long silence. She was probably expecting a reaction, but Maigret was an inert mass.

'I'll tell the consul these people behaved like savages. He knows me. Everyone knows Helen. I'll tell him that they hit me, and that one of the inspectors even felt me up.'

She must have been beautiful once. Now fifty, or maybe fifty-five, she still had a certain style. Was she drunk, or half-drunk, when Maigret had burst into her guesthouse? Perhaps, it was hard to tell. She had that hoarse voice of women who drink and stay up every night, the same slightly blurry look.

It was strange seeing her remain sullenly silent for several minutes, then suddenly mutter something, something short mainly, without appearing to say it to anyone in particular.

'I'll say they hit someone when he was on the ground . . .'

She might have been just venting her anger bit by bit, but then again she might also have been trying to make Maigret blow his top.

'Some people think they're the cream of the crop because they can put an innocent woman in handcuffs.'

It was sometimes so comical that the driver found it hard not to smile.

Maigret, meanwhile, took short puffs on his pipe and tried to keep a straight face.

'I bet they won't even give me a cigarette . . .'

He didn't bat an eyelid, which forced her to take him to task directly.

'Do you have a cigarette, then?'

'Sorry, I didn't know you were talking to me. I don't have one on me, no, I only smoke a pipe. But as soon as we arrive, I'll get one for you.'

The silence this time lasted until Pont de la Jatte.

'They think the French are the only people in this world with a brain. Still, if Larner hadn't told them . . .'

This time, Maigret looked at her in the dim light from the dashboard, but he couldn't decipher any expression on her face. For a while he wondered if she had done it intentionally or not.

The fact was that, with a brief remark, she had just given him an important piece of information. He had suspected as much, in fact. From the start, he had had a feeling that Bill Larner hadn't willingly collaborated with people like

Charlie and Cicero. Besides, his role seemed to be limited to getting them a car, searching Lognon's papers on Place Constantin-Pecqueur and being the driver, taking them first to one of his friends in Rue Brunel and probably then on to the Bon Vivant.

When Lognon had been taken to the forest, Bill had translated but he hadn't been violent.

That night, he must have taken advantage of the fact Charlie had gone back to Paris, leaving him alone with Cicero, to regain the freedom he had been craving for a long time, especially since the business had got too hot for him.

Had he told Cicero he was intending to leave? Had Cicero caught him as he was leaving and tried to stop him? Bill Larner, in any case, had hit him. In the face.

'Do you have a car?' Maigret asked the woman.

Helen clammed up now he was questioning her and reverted to a look of contempt.

He didn't remember seeing a garage near the guest-house. Charlie had left for Paris in the car that they had used to get to Maisons-Laffitte. So Larner must have gone off into the forest on foot, towards the main road or the station. He was now at least two hours ahead of them, and there was little chance they'd catch him before he got over the border.

As they passed an already open bistro at Porte Maillot, Helen declared, still without addressing anyone in particular:

'I'm thirsty.'

'There's cognac in my office. We'll be there in ten minutes.'

The car drove fast through the deserted streets. Some early risers were starting to appear on the pavements. When they stopped at Quai des Orfèvres, in the courtyard of the Palais de Justice, before moving from her seat, Helen asked:

'Will I really get some cognac?'

'I promise.'

Maigret heaved a sigh of relief because he had wondered for a moment if he was going to have to carry her as before in the forest.

'Stay here,' he said to his driver.

When he tried to help the woman up the stairs, she snapped:

'Don't touch me! I'll tell them you tried to sleep with me too.'

Maybe she was only playing a role. Maybe she spent her whole time playing a role to help her cope with her life.

'This way . . .'

'Cognac?'

'Yes . . .'

He pushed open the door of the inspector's office. Torrence and his prisoner hadn't arrived yet because they'd had to stop at Beaujon to drop off the wounded man. Vacher was in there, on the phone, and he gave the American woman a curious look.

'You say that the receiver is off the hook? You're sure? Thank you.'

'Just a moment,' Maigret put in as Vacher opened his mouth. 'Watch her, will you?'

He went into his office, got the bottle of cognac and some glasses and gave Helen a drink, who drained it in one and gestured to the bottle again.

'Not too much at a time. See you in a moment. Do you have any cigarettes, Vacher?'

He put one between the woman's lips and held out a lit match. Blowing smoke into his face, she said:

'I hate you all the same!'

'Haven't you got anyone who can watch her? We'd better not talk too much in front of her.'

'Why not put her in the box room?'

It was over the stairs, a narrow cell with just a bench and a straw mattress. It was dark in there. Maigret hesitated, then decided to put the prisoner in an empty office and lock the door.

'The cognac?' she reminded him through the door.

'Later.'

He rejoined Vacher.

'Whose telephone is off the hook?'

'The Baron's. I have been calling his number pretty much every half hour. Until an hour ago, it rang but no one answered. In the last hour I've been getting the "engaged" buzz. I got worried after a while and rang the supervisor. She says the receiver's off the hook.'

'Do you know where he lives?'

'Rue des Batignolles. The number is written on my pad. Are you going to go?'

'I'd better. Meanwhile, put out the word about Bill Larner. He left Maisons-Laffitte about three hours ago. I think the Belgian border needs watching in particular.

Torrence is going to show up any moment with Tony Cicero.'

'What about the other one?'

'In Beaujon.'

'Did you work him over?'

'Not too badly.'

'What have they said?'

'Nothing.'

Cocking their ears, they looked at one another, then Maigret made for the office in which he had locked Helen. Despite the handcuffs, she was wreaking havoc, sending the inkwells, desk lamp, papers and everything in her reach crashing on to the floor.

When she saw Maigret, she just smiled, saying:

'I'm behaving pretty much as you did at my place.'

'The box room?' asked Vacher.

'It's what she wants.'

On the Pont-Neuf, his car passed the one carrying Torrence and Cicero, and the drivers waved to each other. When he got to Rue des Batignolles, Maigret saw a convertible parked half on the pavement. Looking inside, he read the Baron's name on the little nameplate, which had a Saint Christopher medal on top.

He rang the bell. The concierge, who was still half asleep, unlatched the outer door, and he had to talk to her through the glass panel of the door to find out what floor the inspector lived on.

'Did he come in on his own?' he asked.

'What difference is that to you?'

'I work with him.'

'He can tell you what he did himself.'

It was one of those buildings with several, mainly working-class families on each floor, and lights could already be seen in various apartments. The contrast between this very modest block and the aristocratic appearance the Baron affected was striking, and Maigret now understood why the inspector, a confirmed bachelor, never mentioned his private life.

On the fourth floor, a visiting card with only his name – no mention of his profession – was stuck to the door. Maigret knocked and got no reply. He turned the handle just in case.

The door opened, and he found the Baron's hat on the floor. He switched on the light and saw a tiny kitchen off to the left, then a Renaissance Revival dining room with doilies, the sort you still see in concierge's lodges, and finally a bedroom with the door wide open.

The Baron was sprawled fully dressed across the bed, one arm hanging over the side. If he hadn't been snoring, you might have thought something had happened to him.

'Baron! Hey! Old friend . . .'

He turned over completely without waking up, and Maigret kept on shaking him.

'It's me, Maigret . . .'

This took several minutes. Finally the inspector grunted, half-opened his eyes and moaned because the light was too bright. He recognized Maigret's face and, with a jolt of something like terror, tried to sit up.

'What day is it?'

He had probably meant to ask, 'What time is it?' because he was looking around for the alarm clock which had fallen on the floor. Its ticking was audible from under the bed.

'Do you want a glass of water?'

Maigret went to fetch one from the kitchen and when he came back, he found the inspector looking morose and anxious in equal measure.

'I'm sorry . . . Thank you . . . I'm ill . . . If you only knew how sick I feel . . .'

'Maybe I should make you a strong coffee?'

'I feel ashamed . . . I swear that . . .'

'Stay lying down for a moment.'

The apartment looked more like a spinster's than a bachelor's, and it was easy to imagine the Baron, after a day's work, donning an apron to do the housework.

When he came back in this time, Maigret found the inspector sitting on the edge of the bed, a look of despair in his eyes.

'Drink this . . . You'll feel better afterwards . . .'

He had poured himself a cup of coffee too. Taking off his overcoat, he sat down on a chair. A terrible stench of alcohol filled the room. The inspector's clothes were dirty and crumpled, as if he had spent the night under a bridge.

'It's terrible,' he sighed.

'What's terrible?'

'I don't know. I've got important things to tell you. *Crucial* things.'

'Yes?'

'I'm trying to remember. What's happened?'

'We've arrested Charlie and Cicero.'

'You've arrested them?'

His whole face betrayed effort.

'I don't think I've ever been as drunk in my whole life. I really feel ill. It's something to do with them. Hang on, I remember that we're not supposed to arrest them.'

'Why?'

'Harry told me . . .'

The name had just come back to him, which he considered a victory.

'He's called Harry . . . Wait . . .'

'I'll help you. You were at the Manhattan, Rue des Capucines. You talked to several people and you drank a lot . . .'

'Not at Luigi's. At Luigi's I had hardly anything to drink. It was afterwards . . .'

'Did they make you drink on purpose?'

'I don't know. I'm sure that it will all come back to me bit by bit. He told me that we mustn't arrest them because it might . . . For crying out loud! It's so difficult . . .'

'It might what? You left Luigi's very late. Your car was at the door. You got into it, presumably intending to go to Maisons-Laffitte.'

'How do you know?'

'Someone during the evening, probably Lope or Teddy . . . Brown.'

'Damn, how do you know all this? I did talk to them, I remember now. You put me on to it. I'd already been to quite a few bars.'

'Where you'd had a drink.'

'A glass here, a glass there. You can't do it any other way. I can't feel my head any more.'

'Wait.'

Maigret went into the bathroom and came back out with a towel soaked in cold water, which he put on the Baron's forehead.

'They told you about Helen Donahue and her guest-house in the forest, Au Bon Vivant.'

The Baron stared at him wide-eyed.

'What time is it?'

'Five thirty in the morning.'

'How did you find out?'

'It doesn't matter. When you left Luigi's and got into your car, someone followed you, a man with blond hair, very tall, youngish. He must have approached you.'

'That's right. He's called Harry.'

'Harry who?'

'He told me. I'm sure he told me, I'm even sure it's a one-syllable name. A singer's name.'

'Is he a singer?'

'No, but he's got a singer's name. Before I had time to shut the door, he sat down next to me saying, "Don't be afraid."'

'In French?'

'He spoke French with a heavy accent and made lots of mistakes, but you could understand what he was saying.'

'American?'

'Yes. Wait. Then he said: "I'm sort of police. Don't stay here. Drive. Wherever you like."'

'Then, as soon as I'd started the engine, he explained that he was an assistant district attorney. A district attorney is apparently a sort of examining magistrate and public prosecutor rolled into one. In the big cities they have several assistants.'

'I know.'

'That's right, you've been there. He asked me to stop so he could show me his passport. When it's an important case, the district attorney and his assistants conduct the investigation themselves. Is that right?'

'Correct.'

'He knew where I was heading when I left Luigi's bar. "You mustn't go to Maisons-Lafitte tonight. Nothing good will come of it. I need to talk to you first."'

'Did he?'

'We chatted for at least two hours, but that's the hard bit for me to remember. First we carried on driving aimlessly round the streets, and he gave me a cigar. Maybe it was the cigar that made me want to throw up? I got thirsty. I didn't know where we were but I saw a bistro open. I think it was near Gare du Nord.'

'You didn't tell him to come and see me at headquarters?'

'I did. He didn't want to.'

'Why not?'

'It's complicated. If only my head didn't hurt so badly! Do you think a glass of beer would do me any good?'

'Have you got some beer?'

'There's some on the windowsill outside the kitchen.'

Maigret had some as well. Baron, disgusted by the mess in his bedroom, had dragged himself into the dining room.

'I remember some details very clearly. There are whole sentences I could repeat but, in between, complete blanks.'

'What did you drink?'

'Everything.'

'Him too?'

'He went through the bottles behind the bar and chose.'

'Are you sure he drank as much as you?'

'More. He was really drunk. At one point he fell off his chair.'

'You haven't explained why he refused to get in touch with me.'

'He knows you, actually, and he admires you.'

'Really.'

'He even met you at a cocktail party that was given for you in St Louis and he remembers a sort of talk you gave. He came to France to look for Sloppy Joe.'

'Did he pick him up in Rue Fléchier?'

'Yes.'

'What did he do with him?'

'He took him to a doctor. Wait, don't say anything! A whole chunk's coming back to me. To do with the doctor. He told me how he got to know this doctor. It was immediately after the liberation. Harry, who was in the American army, belonged to some service or other that was stationed in Paris for over a year. He had a whale of a time. One of the people he met was a doctor. That's it! It was through a girl who was afraid she was pregnant and . . .'

'Abortion?'

'Yes. He couldn't even say the word. He is very prudish. I understood anyway. It was a young doctor, just starting out, lives near Boulevard Saint-Michel.'

'Did Harry get Sloppy Joe treated there?'

'Yes. I had the feeling he was telling me the truth. He kept saying. "Tell Maigret this . . . And this."'

'It would have been easier coming here.'

'He didn't want to have any official contact with the French police.'

'Why?'

'It seemed very straightforward last night. I remember agreeing with him. Now it's not so simple. Ah, that's it. First because you would have had to question the wounded man, and it would have been in the papers.'

'Does Harry know that Cinaglia and Cicero are in Paris?'

'He knows everything. He knows them inside out. He found out they were hiding at the Bon Vivant before I did.'

'Does he know Bill Larner?'

'Yes. I think I'm beginning to piece the story together. You see, we were both drunk. He kept repeating himself as if he thought that, being French, I wouldn't understand.'

'I know just what you mean.'

Like Pozzo! Like Luigi!

'There's a big investigation going on in St Louis. One of their periodic attempts to purge the city of its gangsters. Harry is more or less in charge. Everyone knows the man running the rackets, he told me his name, someone with influence – he looks just like a respectable citizen and is friends with the politicians and heads of police.'

'The usual story.'

'That's what he told me. Except that they have different laws over there, and it's difficult to get someone convicted. Is that true?'

'It is.'

'No one dares give evidence against the guy because anyone who opens his mouth has got less than forty-eight hours to live.'

The Baron was very pleased. He had just remembered a good stretch in one go.

'Can I have another glass of beer? It's doing me good. Do you want one?'

He was still looking pasty, with bags under his eyes, but a little spark was starting to flicker in his pupils.

'We went somewhere else because our bistro shut. I don't remember where – in Montmartre probably. A little nightclub where there were three or four dancers. A little brunette gave him the eye and sat on his knee the whole time. We were the only ones there.'

'Did he talk about Sloppy Joe?'

'That's what I'm trying to remember. Sloppy Joe is a sad case, in the last stages of TB. He has spent his whole life racketeering but he's just a stooge. Two months ago a man was murdered in St Louis outside a nightclub. If only I could remember names! Everyone is convinced it's the guy I told you about just now who killed him. There were only two witnesses to the murder, one being the nightclub doorman, who was found dead the next morning in his bedroom. That was when Sloppy Joe went on the run, because he was the second witness, and that is always a risky thing to be.'

'In Canada?'

'In Montreal, yes. On the one hand, the district attorney's office was trying to get their hands on him to make him talk; on the other, the gangsters were anxious to find him to make sure he didn't.'

'I understand.'

'I don't. Apparently Sloppy Joe really represents millions. If he talks, a whole criminal organization and a powerful political machine will collapse. I can still hear Harry telling me: "You don't have those things here. You don't have these wide-ranging criminal conspiracies, organized like corporations. You've got it easy . . ."'

Maigret thought he could hear him too. It was becoming a familiar refrain.

'In Montreal, Sloppy Joe didn't feel there was enough distance between him and his fellow countrymen. He managed to get a fake passport. As the passport was in the name of a couple, he arranged for a woman to accompany him, thinking that would throw the people looking for him even more off the scent. He persuaded a cigarette seller in a nightclub to go with him. She had dreamed of seeing Paris all her life . . . Excuse me for a moment.'

Baron dragged himself to the bathroom, then came back with two aspirins.

'Sloppy Joe didn't have much money. He understood that, even in Paris, they'd get him in the end. So one day he sent a long letter to the district attorney saying that if they promised to protect him, if they came and got him here and if they gave him a certain sum, he would agree to testify. I might be muddling some of it up, but that's the general gist.'

'Did Harry tell you to explain all this to me?'

'Yes. He almost called you. He would have done this morning, if he hadn't realized yesterday that I had discovered the killers' hideout. Because these are real killers, especially Charlie.'

'How did Charlie and Cicero pick up Sloppy Joe's trail?'

'In Montreal. Through the girl Mascarelli took with him. She has a mother there and she was stupid enough to write to her from Paris.'

'Giving an address?'

'A poste restante, but she added that she lived just opposite a big music hall. When Harry decided to set off to collect Sloppy Joe and bring him back to St Louis, he learned that Cinaglia and Cicero had left forty-eight hours earlier.'

Maigret couldn't help picturing poor Mascarelli's existence since leaving St Louis – his life in Montreal, then in Paris, where he hardly dared to leave his hotel for a few minutes in the evening to get some fresh air.

Now he understood why Cicero and Charlie needed a hire car. For two or three days, they had probably been on the watch near the Folies-Bergère, waiting for the right moment to act. When it had finally arrived, the assistant district attorney was on their heels.

'Harry described the scene, it was like something out of a movie. He was on foot. He had just turned the corner of Rue Richer when he saw Sloppy Joe getting into a car. He realized what was up. There was no taxi in sight, so he looked for an unlocked car in front of the theatre.'

It was pretty comical imagining the assistant district attorney in a stolen car! These people, whatever side of the fence they were on, behaved in Paris as if they were at home. The crowd in the streets on Monday had no idea they were witnessing a Chicago-style chase. And if it wasn't for poor Lognon, huddled by the fence of Notre-Dame-de-Lorette, busy with a small-time cocaine dealer, no one would ever have known what they were doing.

'Is Sloppy Joe dead?'

'No. As Harry put it, his doctor is "patching him up". He needed a transfusion, and Harry gave God knows how much of his own blood. He's watching at his bedside like a brother, better than a brother in fact. Apparently his whole career depends on it. If he gets to St Louis with Sloppy Joe alive, if he can keep him breathing until the day of the trial and if the man then repeats his testimony without losing his nerve, Harry will be almost as famous as Dewey when he cleaned up New York's gangland.'

'What about the woman? Did Harry abduct her?'

'Yes. He was angry with you when he saw the photograph of Charlie and Cicero in newspapers.'

These people were all equally serious, you had to give them that, the assistant district attorneys just as much as the killers. It had occurred to them all that Mascarelli's companion might react when she saw the photographs and might decide to go to the police. Which she had in fact done by sending the express letter to Maigret. Charlie had left the Bon Vivant on his own to shut her up. But a few minutes before he got there Harry had collected her and taken her somewhere safe.

Nothing threw them! They just went about their business as if Paris was a sort of no man's land where they could do whatever they pleased.

'Is she at the doctor's too?'

'Yes.'

'Isn't Harry afraid Charlie will find out where he lives?'

'He has taken precautions, apparently. When he goes there, he makes sure he's not followed and he's got someone guarding them.'

'Who?'

'I don't know.'

'All in all, what message exactly did he tell you to give me?'

'He's asking you not to do anything about Charlie and Cicero, at least for a few days. Sloppy Joe won't be moveable for a week. Harry plans to take him to America by plane. It's still dangerous until then.'

'If I understand correctly, he's telling me this is none of my business?'

'More or less. He admires you a great deal and when this is all over he's looking forward to talking to you here or in St Louis.'

'He's too kind! Where did you leave this individual?'

'Outside his hotel.'

'Do you remember the address?'

'It's somewhere around Rue de Rennes. I think if I was there I'd recognize the façade.'

'Do you feel up to coming?'

'Do you mind if I change?'

It would be light soon. People were coming and going in the building, and somewhere a radio was broadcasting the news. Maigret heard the inspector splashing about in the bathroom, and when he came back into the dining room, he looked like a picture in a fashion magazine, except for his complexion, which was still the colour of papier-mâché.

He seemed humiliated at the sight of his car up on the pavement.

'Do you want me to drive?'

'I'd rather take a taxi. But you can park your car properly.'

They walked to Boulevard des Batignolles, where they found a cab.

'Left Bank. Go to Rue de Rennes first.'

'What number?'

'Drive along the whole street.'

They roamed around the neighbourhood for a good quarter of an hour while the Baron inspected the façades of all the hotels. Finally he said:

'It's here.'

'Are you sure?'

'I recognize the brass plate by the door.'

They went in. A man was running a damp cloth over the lobby.

'Is there anyone in the office?'

'The owner only comes down at eight. I'm the night porter.'

'Do you know the names of the guests?'

'They are on the board.'

'Is there an American, a tall, blond-haired guy, youngish, whose first name is Harry?'

'Definitely not.'

'You don't want to check?'

'No point. I know who you're talking about.'

'What?'

'The guy who came in about four thirty this morning. He asked me what room Monsieur Durand was in. I told him we don't have any Durands staying. "How about Dupont?" he said. I thought he was making fun of me so I gave him a filthy look, especially because he seemed totally drunk.'

Maigret and Baron exchanged glances.

'He was standing where you are and didn't seem in a hurry to leave. Then he rummaged around in his pocket and ended up giving me a thousand-franc note and explaining that it was a joke. A woman was after him, and he had come into the hotel to shake her off. He asked me to look in the street and check there weren't any cars around. He stayed another few minutes, then he went off again.'

The Baron was furious.

'He tricked me!' he spat once they were in the street. 'Do you think he's really an assistant district attorney?'

'Most probably.'

'Then why did he do that?'

'Because,' Maigret said calmly as he got into the taxi, 'these people, good and bad alike, think we're children. Not yet out of kindergarten, you know.'

'Where shall I take you now, Monsieur Maigret?' asked the driver, who recognized him.

'Quai des Orfèvres.'

Then he settled back into his corner with a surly shrug.

9.

In which, despite everything, Maigret accepts a glass of whiskey

'The commissioner's just arrived, sir.'

'I'll go and see him.'

It was nine in the morning, and in the grey light Maigret's cheeks were dark with stubble, his eyes faintly red-rimmed. For a good half-hour he had been holding his handkerchief in his hand, because he was tired of taking it out of his pocket every minute.

On three separate occasions someone had come to tell him:

'The woman's kicking up a hell of a racket.'

'Let her.'

Then an inspector had announced:

'I opened the door a crack to give her a cup of coffee, and she threw it in my face. The mattress has been ripped open, and there's straw everywhere.'

He had shrugged. A call had been made to Lucas on his behalf telling him he didn't need to stay at the Bon Vivant any longer.

'Tell him to go to bed!'

But Lucas, who wanted to see it through, had hurried to Quai des Orfèvres with a five o'clock shadow as well.

As for Torrence, he had shut himself away in an office with Tony Cicero. He persisted in asking the American questions which elicited nothing but a contemptuous silence.

'You're wasting your time, my friend,' Maigret had remarked.

'I know, but I enjoy it. He doesn't understand a word I'm saying, but I can see it's worrying him. He's desperate for a cigarette but he's too proud to ask for one. He'll come round. He's already opened his mouth once and then shut it again without saying anything.'

There was a strange excitement in the air that only Maigret's few close collaborators on the case could understand. Young Lapointe, for example, who was none the wiser when he got to the office, wondered why Maigret and his men were throwing themselves into their strange tasks this morning with such a will.

They had primed the fifth and sixth arrondissement police stations.

'A doctor, yes, probably quite young. He lives near Boulevard Saint-Michel, but I don't think he'll have a sign outside his door. The local women will know him, because he does abortions occasionally. Question the local chemists. He probably bought a fair amount of medicine last Tuesday. Go round the companies selling surgical instruments too.'

This morning all the local inspectors who knew about the case were going from door to door, from chemist to chemist, without suspecting they were dealing with people who had come from St Louis to settle their scores.

Another inspector from the Police Judiciaire was at the School of Medicine, copying out lists of students who had completed PhDs in recent years. Others were questioning the teachers. The Vice Squad was frantically busy, waking unsuspecting working girls.

'Ever had an abortion?'

'Honestly! Who do you take me for?'

'All right, all right! We're not trying to cause you problems. There's a doctor around here who'll take care of all that. Who is it?'

'I only know a midwife. Have you asked Sylvie?'

If you included the border police and the gendarmes out on the roads watching for Bill Larner, several hundred people had been mobilized for the Americans' sake.

Maigret knocked on a door, closed it behind him, shook hands with the commissioner of the Police Judiciaire and sank into a chair. For ten minutes he detailed everything he knew about the case in a monotone.

By the end, the commissioner seemed more embarrassed than him.

'What do you plan to do? Get your hands on this Mascarelli?'

Maigret was tempted. He had had it with being treated like a child.

'If I do, I'll stop the assistant district attorney catching his crime boss.'

'And if you don't you won't be able to charge Charlie and Cicero with attempted murder.'

'Obviously. Which leaves Lognon. They *kidnapped*, as they say over there, Lognon and took him to Saint-Germain forest, where they beat him up. They also broke into his home and finally Charlie shot a policeman in Rue Grange-Batelière.'

'He'll claim he was attacked or thought there was an ambush, and it does look that way. His lawyer will say that he was walking peaceably down the street when he saw two men about to jump him.'

'Fine! Let's suppose that's how it is. We still have Lognon, and that will get them several years inside, or at the very least several months.'

The commissioner couldn't help smiling at the stubborn expression on Maigret's face.

'The woman's got nothing to do with Lognon's business,' he objected again.

'I know. We'll have to let her go. That's why I'm letting her scream. I can't do anything against Pozzo either. We'll catch him out one of these days and shut down his club.'

'Angry, Maigret?'

It was Maigret's turn to smile.

'Admit it, chief, they're pushing it. If Lognon hadn't gone above and beyond on that Monday night, everything would have happened right under our noses. They would have told the story later in St Louis. I can hear someone ask: "What about the French police?" "The French police? They didn't have a clue, the French police . . . What do you expect?"'

It was eleven, and Maigret had just replied to Madame Lognon's questions – her second call of the day – when an inspector from the sixth arrondissement rang him.

'Hello, Detective Chief Inspector Maigret? The doctor's called Louis Duvivier and he lives at 17A, Rue Monsieur-le-Prince.'

'Is he at home now?'

'Yes.'

'Is there anyone with him?'

'The concierge thinks that a sick man's been staying in his apartment for several days. She was surprised by that because usually he only has women patients. It's true that there's a woman staying there as well.'

'How long?'

'Since yesterday.'

'No one else?'

'An American visits almost daily.'

Maigret hung up and a quarter of an hour later he was slowly climbing the stairs in the doctor's building. It was an old apartment block without a lift, and the man's apartment was on the sixth floor. A rope hung to the left of the door. When he pulled it he heard footsteps inside. Then the door opened a crack, and he glimpsed a face. Pushing the door open with his foot, he grunted:

'What are you doing here?'

He wanted to burst out laughing. The guy standing there, pistol in hand, was none other than a fellow called Dédé-de-Marseille, who threw his weight around in the clubs in Rue de Douai. Dédé didn't know what to say and just looked wide-eyed at Maigret as he tried to hide his gun.

'I'm not doing anything wrong, I promise.'

'Hello, Monsieur Maigret!'

The tall blond-haired American in shirt-sleeves came out of an attic room with a sloping ceiling and a skylight like an artist's studio.

His face was a little puffy, his eyes blurry like the Baron's, but the expression on his face was gleeful. He held out a hand.

'I thought I might have said too much and that you'd end up finding out the address. Are you furious with me?'

A young woman came out of the kitchen, where she was making something on a portable stove.

'Can I introduce you?'

'I'd rather you and I went downstairs.'

He had glimpsed a bed with someone in it, a man with brown hair who was trying to hide.

'I understand. Wait a minute.'

He soon reappeared with a jacket and a hat.

'What shall I do?' Dédé asked him, although he was also addressing Maigret.

'Whatever you like,' answered Maigret. 'The guys are behind bars.'

On the stairs, Maigret and his companion didn't say anything. Outside, they began to walk towards Boulevard Saint-Michel.

'Is it true what you just said?'

'About Cicero, yes. Charlie's in hospital.'

'Did your inspector give you my message?'

'How soon can you take the plane with your charge?'

'Three or four days. It'll depend on the doctor. Are you going to make life hard for him?'

'Tell me, Monsieur Harry . . . Harry what?

'Pills.'

'That's it. Like the singer! That's what Baron told me. Suppose I go to your country and carry on the way you've carried on here?'

'Point taken.'

'You haven't answered.'

'You'd be asking for trouble, big trouble.'

'Where did you get to know Dédé?'

'After the Liberation, when I spent most of my nights in the clubs of Montmartre.'

'Did you hire him to guard the wounded man?'

'I couldn't stay in the apartment round the clock. Nor could the doctor.'

'What are you going to do with the woman?'

'She hasn't got any money to go back. I'm buying her a ticket. She's taking a boat the day after tomorrow.'

They were in front of a bar. Harry Pills stopped and muttered tentatively:

'You don't think we could have a drink, do you? I mean, would you allow me to . . .'

It was funny seeing this tall athletic lad blushing like that fool Lognon.

'They may not have any whiskey,' objected Maigret.

'They do. I know for a fact.'

He ordered, then raised his glass, holding it out in front of him for a moment. Maigret gave him a surly look, like a man who still holds a grudge, and said in an ambiguous tone:

'To Gay Paris, as you call it.'

'Still angry?'

Perhaps because he wanted to show that he was not as angry as all that, or because Pills was a likeable fellow, Maigret had a second drink. And as he could not leave without standing a round, a third followed.

'Listen, Maigret, my friend . . . .'

'No, Harry, I'm the one doing the talking . . .'

Around midday Pills said:

'You see, Jules . . .'

'What's the matter with you?' asked Madame Maigret. 'You seem . . .'

'I've just got a cold. I'm off to bed with a hot toddy and two aspirins.'

'Aren't you having anything to eat?'

He crossed the dining room without answering, went into his bedroom and began to undress. If it weren't for his wife, he probably would have gone to sleep in his socks.

Still, he had shown them . . . Absolutely!

INSPECTOR MAIGRET

OTHER TITLES IN THE SERIES

THE CELLARS OF THE MAJESTIC
GEORGES SIMENON

'Try to imagine a guest, a wealthy woman, staying at the Majestic with her husband, her son, a nurse and a governess... At six in the morning, she's strangled, not in her room, but in the basement locker room.'

Below stairs at a glamorous hotel on the Champs-Élysèes, the workers' lives are worlds away from the luxury enjoyed by the wealthy guests. When their worlds meet, Maigret discovers a tragic story of ambition, blackmail and unrequited love.

Translated by Howard Curtis

Other Titles in the Series

THE JUDGE'S HOUSE
GEORGES SIMENON

'He went out, lit his pipe and walked slowly to the harbour. He could hear scurrying footsteps behind him. The sea was becoming swollen. The beams of the lighthouses joined in the sky. The moon had just risen and the judge's house emerged from the darkness, all white, a crude, livid, unreal white.'

Exiled from the Police Judiciare in Paris, Maigret bides his time in a remote coastal town in France. There, among the lighthouses, mussel farms and the eerie wail of foghorns, he discovers that a community's loyalties hide unpleasant truths.

Translated by Howard Curtis

OTHER TITLES IN THE SERIES

SIGNED, PICPUS
GEORGES SIMENON

'"It's a matter of life and death!" he said.

A small, thin man, rather dull to look at, neither young nor old, exuding the stale smell of a bachelor who does not look after himself. He pulls his fingers and cracks his knuckles while telling his tale, the way a schoolboy recites his lesson.'

A mysterious note predicting the murder of a fortune-teller; a confused old man locked in a Paris apartment; a financier who goes fishing; a South American heiress... Maigret must make his way through a frustrating maze of clues, suspects and motives to find out what connects them.

Translated by David Coward

OTHER TITLES IN THE SERIES